"Any regrets?" Rennie asked quietly in the car

Oh, Milla had all kinds of regrets. "About what happened in the kitchen?" *When you made love to me...* "No, not at all."

It sounded good. Not very convincing, but mature. Proving to each other they were no longer reckless college kids but responsible adults all grown up.

All grown up indeed, Milla thought. But what do you say to an ex-lover who suddenly wasn't so *ex?*

"That might not have been the smartest thing either of us has ever done," Rennie conceded as he took her hand. "But if we get hung up on it now, it'll be hard to move forward."

Where did he think they were going? Besides out for drinks? "It was just sex, Rennie. Nothing to lose sleep over." *Liar.*

"Right. Sex." He gave a sharp laugh. "It was always about sex with us, wasn't it?"

Milla looked at him. "Actually," she said softly. "That's not how I remember it at all."

Blaze™

Dear Reader,

One of the things I love about writing for the Harlequin Blaze line is working with other authors on miniseries where we use the same settings or borrow one another's characters. The collaboration on FOR A GOOD TIME CALL... began at least two years ago, and went through a number of incarnations before the pitch was presented to the editors.

Crystal Green (*Innuendo* 7/06), Nancy Warren (*Indulge* 9/06) and I had great fun brainstorming—especially since the idea of the "boot" of business cards was one Crystal had seen in practice. What better way to write a fictional miniseries than to base it on real-life events! I love the idea of women recycling their men in order to help out their girlfriends who might be needing a date...or more!

We set our stories in San Francisco, which has so much history along with a romantic atmosphere. That romantic atmosphere made the perfect backdrop for *Infatuation,* the story of ex-lovers who have never been able to let go of what they had together. I hope you enjoy both of Milla and Rennie's stories—current and past!

Best,

Alison Kent

ALISON KENT
Infatuation

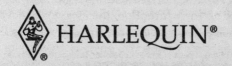

HARLEQUIN®

TORONTO • NEW YORK • LONDON
AMSTERDAM • PARIS • SYDNEY • HAMBURG
STOCKHOLM • ATHENS • TOKYO • MILAN • MADRID
PRAGUE • WARSAW • BUDAPEST • AUCKLAND

ISBN-13: 978-0-373-79291-7
ISBN-10:   0-373-79291-3

INFATUATION

Copyright © 2006 by Mica Stone.

www.eHarlequin.com

Printed in U.S.A.

ABOUT THE AUTHOR

Alison Kent was a born reader, but it wasn't until she reached thirty that she knew she wanted to be a writer when she grew up. Five years later she made her first sale, and hasn't looked back since. With over thirty titles contracted or in print, Alison writes full-time for the Harlequin Blaze line. She is also a partner in Access Romance, an online author community (www.accessromance.com) and DreamForge Media (www.dreamforgemedia.com) as a Web site designer.

Alison lives in a Houston, Texas, suburb with her hero, any number of their four vagabond kids and a dog named Smith. Readers can contact her through her Web site at www.alisonkent.com.

Books by Alison Kent
HARLEQUIN BLAZE

*www.girl-gear...
†Do Not Disturb
**Red Letter Nights

With thanks to Susan Sheppard, Susan Pezzack, Jennifer Green and Birgit Davis-Todd—the Harlequin Blaze editors who have shaped what I've written into the best it can be

1

"MILLA, SWEETIE. Not to be a bitch or anything, but for being the absolutely gorgeous woman that you are? You look like crap today."

Milla Page glared with no small amount of envy at her coworker's mirrored reflection. She and Natalie Tate had taken the elevator from their shared tenth-floor office in San Francisco's Wentworth-Holt building down to the much roomier second-floor ladies' room since theirs was yet again under renovation.

Looking at the other woman's caramel skin, deep coffee-colored hair and vibrant green eyes was a welcome change from Milla's staring at her own reflected deathlike palette of white and, um, even whiter.

That's what she'd been doing now for five minutes at least, staring and wondering what she'd been thinking, letting herself out of the house this morning without so much as a brown paper bag over her head.

"Crap pretty much covers it," she finally replied, sighing heavily. "Though originally I was thinking pasty. Like a ghoul. Or a zombie. Maybe even a corpse."

"Whatever. You're definitely hovering near the

transparent end of the pale scale." Natalie tossed the words over her shoulder, latching the stall door behind her.

Well, yeah. The ghoul-zombie-corpse-pasty-death look would definitely be the wrong end.

This is what happened, Milla mused, when one stayed out too late, ate too much food, drank too much drink, slept too little sleep, did it too often in the company of men who were poster children for singlehood being a good thing, and had to get up the next morning and do it again that night.

What in the world had she been thinking, taking a job with the San Francisco office of MatchMeUpOnline.com that essentially made dating her career? She was a glutton for punishment. There was no other explanation. Dating as recreation was bad enough, all that waxing, shaving, polishing, styling…and for what?

Shaking her head, she reached into her pebbled leather tote for her makeup bag, setting her blush on the restroom's brown marble countertop, and wavering between the soft Sweetie Chic lipstick or the bright Chili Pop. She went with the former, certain the latter would make her look like a fat-lipped bloated clown.

Even though she had lived in San Francisco since graduating from university here six years ago—giving her a decade's worth of experience with the ins and outs of being single in the city by the bay, *and* earning her the Web site's choice restaurant and club review gig—she was still at a clear disadvantage when it came to doing her job.

Basing her thumbs-up or thumbs-down on whether or not the hot spots she was assigned to review worked as locations for intimate dates meant…dating. Dating was hardly a solo gig. Dating meant finding men. And since she hadn't been in a serious relationship since college, finding men meant work.

At least her two female coworkers did what they could to help out. Both Amy Childs and her husband Chris, and Natalie and her fiancé Jamal were good at fixing up Milla with really great guys. When it had become obvious that nothing was going to develop but the shared chemistry of friendship, she kept a couple of the men on the hook for regular dates.

Knowing that she would show them a good time, get them into the toniest of places, *and* pay for the food, how could they say no? And for Milla, it seemed so much easier to deal with the sure thing than with the iffy.

Unfortunately, it also defeated the purpose of what she'd been assigned to do. Gauging a club's up-close-and-personal potential with a man who was only a friend didn't always provide her reviews the same zing as would a more, uh, heated encounter.

Then again, if taking that leap into the unknown as she'd done last night was going to mean dragging into work the next day with a ghoul-zombie-corpselike pallor, *fuggetaboutit!* Except now that she'd been given this newest assignment—the best sort of challenge, her boss, Joan Redmond, called it…Milla groaned, and called it pure torture.

For the next three Friday nights before they headed into the Thanksgiving holiday, she would be torturing herself in a coordinated endeavor with her online counterparts in Seattle, Denver, Austin, Miami and Atlanta as each checked out three new properties in their respective cities. The clubs and restaurants on each city's list had purportedly been designed to ensure couples complete privacy, offering an *anything goes* atmosphere.

Milla had not been told that her job was on the line, but the undercurrent was there. Office scuttlebutt had it that the Web site's advertisers weren't happy with Joan's safe, middle-of-the road approach to showcasing the city. They wanted a November full of action. They wanted sex appeal. They wanted heat and steam and the rawest of exposés.

That meant they wanted Milla. And right now, all Milla wanted to do was to go home to bed. Alone.

The thought of spending three weekends in a row reviewing a particularly sizzling singles' scene held zero appeal. In fact, the only thing keeping her from telling Joan she just couldn't do it and walking off the job was that her date for tomorrow was Chad Rogers, one of the good friends she'd made through Natalie and Jamal. Whether or not Chad could make the next two weeks was still up in the air.

Natalie flushed, heading from the stall to the sink. She washed her hands, studying Milla's mirror image with concern while drying. The look was hardly encouraging.

"Let me see what you've got in that bag," Natalie said once she'd tossed the paper towels in the trash and plucked the lipsticks from Milla's grasp.

At this point, Milla was just tired enough to hand over the management of her entire existence to her trusted friend. Starting with her makeup could not be a bad idea; there was a reason Natalie was in charge of the Web site's fashion pages. Today she appeared to have stepped out of a Salvador Dali canvas—and she made the rather surreal look work.

"So, tell me about last night," she said, digging through Milla's things and coming up with her eyeshadow quad.

Had Milla even remembered eyeshadow this morning? She closed her eyes at the wave of Natalie's hand. "It was a new Italian place and had the potential to be very romantic. Soft music. One small lamp hanging over each table. And gorgeous floral watercolors."

"But?" Natalie smoothed the pad of her thumb over Milla's eyelid to blend the shadow she'd brushed on.

"The tables were practically on top of one another." She backed away to sneeze, and at her girlfriend's "Bless you" said, "Thanks. Anyway. Good food and quiet conversation, yes. Under the table hanky panky, no."

"I don't care about the food or the ambience," Natalie said, moving from Milla's right eye to her left. "That's your job, not mine. I want to know about your date. Was he one of the recycled men?"

Milla smiled as she did every time Natalie used the

expression to refer to the dating pool created by the single women in the building's various offices. It was in the lounge off this very restroom, in fact, where the Sisters of the Booty Call held their Monday lunch-hour meetings. Milla remembered her very first one, and how intrigued she'd been by what sounded like an urban legend but turned out to be true.

Pamela Hoff, the regal blond financial consultant from the building's fifteenth floor, was the mastermind behind the tradition. After a streak of bad dating luck had ended with a night out in the company of an uncouth John Wayne-loving buffoon, she'd considered celibacy as an option to finding a suitable man.

Instead when after a lengthy phone harassment campaign he'd arrived in person to see if she'd received his flowers, she'd taken a more proactive approach to the problem, tucking the bouquet into his pants and adding the water from the vase to let him know she meant business.

Giving the cowboy the boot had been a liberating experience. Pamela had determined then and there that the women in the building had to watch one another's backs, and the dating service was born.

Now, the original etched-glass vase shaped like a boot sat on the center of the lounge's mahogany coffee table. Any woman who wanted to participate would drop into the boot the business card of a man she'd gone out with, one with whom she hadn't personally clicked but one who had promise.

She would also write a descriptive note on the back,

telling the sisters a little bit about the man. When it was her turn to need a date, she'd draw a card from the impressive collection. It was a good way to weed out the scum and the sleaze, and to prescreen prospective dates.

But it was not a guaranteed road to romance as Milla had been made well aware of last night.

"Well?" Natalie prompted. "And you can open your eyes."

Milla did, watching the other woman pull concealer and a blush from the bag. "I tossed the card. Another round of recycling will only get up too many hopes. His, and some poor unsuspecting sister's."

"If he was such a loser, what was he doing in the boot to begin with?" Natalie asked, blotting concealer over the dark circles beneath Milla's eyes.

"One of the girls from the travel agency, I think it was Jo Ann, dropped him in," Milla said, looking up at the ceiling while Natalie worked. "She said they met on a tour of a new cruise ship, and he was the life of the party."

Her own fault, really. She should've known better than to call him in the first place since life-of-the-party guys were so not her style. Not anymore. Not since college and the party that had ended four years of romantic bliss. She'd been wounded by the breakup, yes. That didn't make her any more innocent than the other man involved....

Having finished with both sets of eye baggage as well as the blush, Natalie asked, "What do you think?"

Milla turned toward the mirror. Her chunky blond

layers framed her face as always, hanging just beneath her chin and flipping this way and that. The ghoul-zombie-corpse likeness was gone. She still looked tired, but at least now she didn't appear to have fallen from Death's family tree.

"Nat, you are the best." Milla wrapped her arms around her friend and hugged. "Now, if I can make it through today and manage to get a full eight hours tonight, I might actually show Chad a decent time on Friday."

Natalie bowed her head and began packing Milla's makeup. "Uh, about Friday."

Uh-oh. "No. Please. Don't even say it."

"I'm sorry, sweetie. Jamal and Chad both got put into surgery rotation," Natalie explained, zipping the bag and tucking it into Milla's purse. "Jamal sent me a text message just before I headed down here."

"Then that does it. I'll call it off, and spend the weekend sleeping, eating and watching a season or two of my 'Gilmore Girls' DVDs," Milla said with a sigh, dipping a toe into fantasyland before Natalie smacked her back to reality.

The smackdown wasn't long in coming. "Don't make me laugh. You'll tell Joan…what exactly?"

"Joan will understand a last-minute glitch," Milla said, fluffing her hair.

"She might," Natalie said, pointing one finger at Milla's reflection. "Except your last minute glitch has the potential for throwing off the coordination between all the city Web sites involved in this project. And for giving our advertisers even more to bitch about."

Natalie was right, of course. This wasn't just a San Francisco venture. It was part of MatchMeUpOnline.com's master plan for nationwide domination of online dating. Since she benefited in a very nice financial way, Milla appreciated the company's vision. But when putting the plan into practice meant one bad date after another, her appreciation dimmed.

She was damned tired. She hadn't had a real date—a fun, relaxing, nonworking, hot and sexy date—in longer than she could remember. Her social life was getting in the way of her social life, and it stunk. "Okay, Ms. Solutions 'R Us. How am I supposed to find a date on such short notice?"

Natalie frowned. "I thought you had a little black book of sure things."

"I do." Granted, a very *very* little black book. "But if I start using and abusing with this last-minute stuff, how long do you think it's going to be before these guys start changing their numbers?"

"Give me a break," Natalie said with a huff. "For a chance to go out with you? I can't see them caring how much notice you give them."

"You're a sweetheart, Nat." And she really was. But she knew the truth as well as Milla did. "These guys know that going out with me is all about work. Even good friends get tired of the damper that puts on things."

Natalie turned around and leaned against the countertop. "I'm trying to think of anyone else we know, or someone new in Jamal's circle, but I'm coming up blank."

Most of the eligible bachelors Natalie knew worked with Jamal at St. Luke's Hospital. That was how Milla had met Chad, one of her no-strings regulars. She wondered what sort of reputation she had there; if Jamal's friends rolled their eyes or ran screaming into the night every time he drafted them into hooking up.

That was exactly what she didn't want happening. "You know what? Don't worry about it. I'll check with Amy, and if she doesn't have any ideas, I'll call one of the guys in my book. An emergency is an emergency, right?"

"Wait a minute." Natalie pushed away from the countertop. "Correct me if I'm wrong, girlfriend, but aren't we overlooking the obvious here? The stash of names and numbers in that boot in the lounge?"

"Yes, but after last night?" Milla shuddered just thinking about a repeat of that particularly bad experience. "Besides, the tradition is that we get together as a group during Monday's lunch if we're going to dip into the kitty."

"Sure, when you're not strapped for time," Natalie said, arms crossed, hip cocked, brow lifted in that listen-up look she delivered so well. "I may not belong to your club, but I can't see anyone objecting to you making a Thursday booty call seeing as how you're in this bind. Right now, you need to worry about Joan and the advertisers. You get through this Friday, Amy and I will put our heads together and figure out your future."

"I wish you would. I'm obviously having no luck getting anywhere with men on my own." Milla chuckled to herself. "At least not anywhere beyond the best restaurants and clubs in the city."

"Oh, blah, blah, blah, cry me a river already," Natalie said, taking hold of Milla's upper arm and herding her toward the restroom's lounge and the glass boot full of business cards and untapped possibilities. "Pick yourself a good one and hope he's free tomorrow night so those of us with work to do can get back to it."

Milla stuck out her tongue as she settled on the sofa and set her purse on the table next to the vase. She pulled her cell phone from the pouch inside, deciding it would be a waste of time not to call from here, and then she picked a card.

"What does it say?" Natalie asked as Milla silently scanned the note scribbled on the back.

"'Great eyes? Check. Incredible smile? Check. Body to make a girl melt inside? Check, check, check. Potential for high-yield capital gains? No, but he's hell on wheels in bed. And really, isn't that all that *matters?*'"

"See?" Natalie said. "There you go. Who better than a hot body to scope out a hot spot?"

That part Milla couldn't argue with. And since she'd pretty much given up expecting dating to be meaningful or more than the occasional good time, a guy's potential for high-yield capital gains had dropped off her radar.

It was, however, when she turned over the card and

read the name embossed on the front that truth became stranger than fiction. The white rectangle fluttered to the carpet. Natalie bent and picked it up while Milla stared at her fingers that had grown useless and cold.

"'Bergen Motors,'" Natalie read. "'Serving the Bay Area for Forty Years. Rennie Bergen, Sales.'" She tapped her finger along the edge of the card, then stopped as suddenly as she'd started. "You don't think—"

"No. I don't think. I *know*." Rennie Bergen had been her boyfriend Derek's college roommate during his freshman year, and as much a part of Milla's life during that one and the three that had followed as had been research papers and labs.

He'd also been her indiscretion. Her one and only. Over and over and over again.

"Didn't you say he disappeared after graduation?"

So much had happened after graduation, she didn't even know where to begin. "He left the city, yeah. He said he wouldn't be back until he'd made his first million."

"Unless he's selling Lamborghinis, it doesn't look like he met his goal." Natalie started to drop the card back into the glass boot.

Milla snatched it away. Her girlfriend had no way of knowing the full extent of what had gone on with Rennie Bergen. No one knew. Things left unsettled when he vanished without a word. Things for which Milla had never forgiven herself. Things over which she still carried guilt.

Not that she wore those feelings on her sleeve, or

brought them out like voodoo dolls to stick with pins. They were just there, the same way as were the feelings from her past for any of her friends. Only not the same.

Because more than anyone else in her life, she had hurt Rennie Bergen, and she'd never had a chance to make amends.

Well, now she did, and she had to seize the opportunity that had been dropped into her lap. If she continued to leave the past unsettled, she would never forgive herself. She could only hope that after all this time Rennie would be able to forgive her.

"Don't tell me you're going to call him," Natalie said as Milla got to her feet.

She picked up her purse, tucked her phone down inside, dug for her car keys and sunglasses—and she did it all without giving herself time to examine the emotions that were driving her. She was afraid if she looked at them too closely, she'd stop.

"No. I'm going to see him. Tell Joan I'll be back when I'm back," she said, leaving the restroom, heading for the elevator, and praying she wasn't making the second biggest mistake of her life.

"YO, REN. JIN'S ON THE phone. He says the frame's got a nickel-sized rust hole on the cross panel support. He wants to know if he should haggle the Captain on the price since it ain't so pristine as he said."

Son of a barking dog. Rennie Bergen planted the rubber of his heels on the garage's slick concrete floor and rolled the creeper out from beneath the panel van that had once been an ice cream truck. The water pump was pissing like a baby kangaroo. Story of his life.

He got to his feet and looked for Hector who was halfway across the hangar-size building and heading Rennie's way with the phone. If he didn't find a workable frame and soon…aw, hell, who was he kidding?

It wasn't the frame that was the problem. It was the entire concept. Turning a VW bus into a submersible had seemed like such a good idea when he'd been six beers under the table and scrambling for new show ideas.

He grabbed the phone from Hector's hand and yelled at Jin. "You tell the Captain thanks, but no thanks. And if he keeps hitting me with this crap, he can forget seeing another dime of my business, I don't care how long he's known my father."

His voice still echoing, Rennie disconnected before Jin could respond, tossed the phone back to Hector, and headed for the huge stainless-steel sink on the wall outside the office and the john. From the exterior, the garage looked like nothing, a big metal building like any other warehouse or shop. Except it wasn't.

The garage was home to the cable TV phenomenon "Hell on Wheels." The show had made Rennie Bergen a star with a cult following few car buffs could claim. That was because few, if any, managed what he and his crew accomplished, turning passenger vehicles into mechanical wonders such as low-rider school buses and rolling techno clubs.

The best part of his success was that he wasn't a

household name. He could still walk down an average city street and never turn a head. He stood a better chance of being recognized in blue-collar neighborhoods where a man's vehicle of choice was less a reflection of his portfolio or family status and more an extension of his personality.

Rennie had grown up in such a neighborhood. Good people, living and loving paycheck to paycheck, hoping the life they were able to provide their kids would be enough. It had been for Rennie. The summer vacations, the balancing of school and athletics and work, the nightly dinners at seven. The holiday celebrations that included his father's employees and their families—from salesmen to secretaries to grease monkeys—along with the extended Bergen clan.

It had been an insular world of tightly woven bonds, but growing up in that atmosphere had given him an appreciation for men willing to get their hands dirty while taking care of their own. His first real exposure to the flip side hadn't come until his freshman year in college.

While his parents had paid what they could of his fees and tuition, he'd held down a job to pay the rest along with his room and board. Living on campus had been easier than spending valuable study time commuting from home when he worked so close to the school.

But his first-year roommate, Derek Randall, one of the privileged and wealthy big men on campus, had been all about paying other men to do his dirty work while taking care of himself. And Derek's girlfriend, Milla Page…

Rennie shoved off the water and yanked enough paper towels from the dispenser to dry his arms up to his elbows. Derek hadn't been a bad guy, just from a world Rennie hadn't been used to. The fact that they'd butted heads so often had been only the tip of the iceberg Rennie had eventually faced, trying to fit in with that crowd before realizing the futility of the effort.

He'd made his way in the world, and then he'd come home, belonging here, comfortable here, employing men who shared his background and his belief that there was no such thing as a job that was too dirty when a little muscle and degreaser made cleanup a breeze. Still, he had to admit it was a hell of a lot more fun working for the man when he *was* the man and was rolling in a big fat pile of greenbacks.

"Yo, Ren," Hector hollered. "Today just ain't your day, man. Angie called up from the showroom. Some blonde's here to see you."

Rennie tossed the towels in the trash and glanced at Hector who stood in the doorway of the office. The long-time Bergen Motors' employee was Rennie's right hand man. "This blonde got a name? Better yet. Did she bring me a rust-free frame?"

"She didn't even bring much in the way of a female frame, Angie's saying." Hector frowned as he listened to the other end of the phone conversation. "She's like a stick figure with white skin and white hair, and eyes like big green double spoke rims. Her name is—"

"Milla," Rennie said, swallowing hard as his gut drew up into the knot of fiery emotions he hadn't felt in years. "Her name is Milla Page."

2

SHE LOOKED exactly as he remembered. She'd always been slender; it had been an ongoing source of inside jokes, fearing she would snap in a strong wind, be whipped about on the bay's waves like driftwood, float on a bank of misty fog. That she would break in two if he wasn't gentle when they made love.

She'd disabused him of that notion quite forcefully and quite often—often enough that those memories were the first to come to mind when he should have remembered that everything between them had been a lie. Instead, all he could think about was the sex.

She didn't say anything, just stood in front of him, her feet primly together in shoes he knew cost what was a month's rent for Hector, Angie and Jin. He didn't hold it against her. Milla Page was who she was.

He could tell by the way she clenched and unclenched her fingers around the handle of her funky purple purse that he'd been standing and staring way too long.

She was uncomfortable; he gave her the benefit of the doubt, deciding it wasn't the fault of the neighborhood as much as it was seeing him again.

It probably didn't help that Angie sat behind the receptionist station punching buttons on the switchboard console, transferring calls and paging salesmen, glancing back and forth between them while neither one said a word.

So Rennie forced a smile and motioned Milla forward, leading the way across the sales floor to the customer lounge, listening for her soft steps to fall behind him. He grabbed a foam cup from the corner table's stack and poured himself a coffee from the pot on the warmer. Milla shook her head when he offered to pour one for her.

"Still prefer lattes?" he asked, now a fan himself though in a pinch of nerves sludge would do.

"Yes, but right now I don't think I could swallow anything," she replied in that voice that still slid over him like the honey she'd loved…so sticky, so sweet, so warm on her tongue.

He nearly choked as he knocked back a slug of the caffeine. He was already wired to the gills and hardly in need of the jolt, but he wasn't quite sure what to do. And he wouldn't be able to figure that out until he knew what she was doing here.

Why it had taken her six years to look him up.

Why she appeared ready to bolt.

Why he cared when he'd sworn to wipe her from his mind.

Curiosity got the better of his self-made promise. He gestured toward the row of chairs on her right. "Sit. Please."

She did as he'd asked, or rather as he'd ordered her, choosing the seat closest to where she stood and settling onto the edge. She held her purse tightly in her lap.

Her knuckles stood out like bleached bones beneath translucent skin. Her smile seemed forced and fragile, and that made him groan.

No matter her size, Milla Page was the least fragile woman he'd ever known. If anything, she was unbreakable. Untouchable. Unyielding. And he shouldn't be feeling responsible for the change.

He moved closer, choosing to leave only one seat between them and angling his body to the side. He liked the idea of the space between them being more for show than effect. He wanted to see if after all this time he could still make her sweat.

Or if there was more to her emotional state than a simple case of nerves. "I guess this is where we do the small talk thing. Unless you want to skip the catching up and just tell me why you're here."

"I happened—"

He cut her off with a shake of his head and a laugh that was harsh. "Nope. I don't buy that you just happened to be in the neighborhood."

He watched as she struggled not to snap back. Her eyes, as always, gave her away. "What I was going to say was that I happened across your business card."

"So you're here to buy a car?" The more likely scenario was that she was here to see for herself that he really *hadn't* come up in the world.

But she shook her head, surprising him by admitting, "I'm here to see you."

He grunted, slumped back in his chair. Did she know about his show? Had she come thinking to cash in on his celebrity? Was his financial portfolio more to her liking than had been his empty pockets in college?

"It surprised me…seeing your name like that…I hadn't thought of you in years—" She caught herself, her mouth clamping shut on her words. She shook off whatever it was she'd been thinking, and started again. "No. That's not true."

"Which part?" he asked, the words clattering out on a growl. The sound was an echo of the uproar piston-pumping through his midsection. "That seeing my name surprised you when we both know it shouldn't have caused a blip on your radar?"

She set her purse on the seat between them and got to her feet, moving across the room to the coffee service before turning around. "I think about you every day, Rennie. I have for the last six years."

He didn't believe her. Unbreakable, untouchable, and unable to tell the truth when a lie would do. Even worse was knowing all of that and wishing it wasn't so.

Wishing she had thought about him as often as he'd thought about her.

He clenched his fist, felt the foam of his cup begin to give. "So, you think about me every day, but it takes seeing my business card to get you to stop by?"

She shrugged. "I didn't know you'd come back to the city."

That's right. He'd told her he was off to see the world. That he wouldn't return until he'd made his first million. Instead he'd come back after what seemed like a million miles on the road and a million sleepless nights to make his fortune right here at home.

"You could've driven by and asked," he finally said, his jaw tight, shooting his near-empty cup into the brown rubber can in the corner. Drops of coffee spattered across the white liner.

"You're right." She walked back into the room, sat in the chair across from his. "I could have and I didn't. I'm not sure why."

He knew exactly. And he started to remind her of their last night together, the party, the fight that had grown larger than either of them had known what to do with. But the expression of pain on her face stopped him.

He draped his arms over the backs of the seats on either side, stretched out his legs and crossed his ankles. When he rocked his feet, the toe of his boot grazed her lower calf. "I didn't look you up, either. When I got home. Guess that evens the score."

"How long *have* you been back?" she asked softly, looking at his legs rather than meeting his eyes.

Streaks of grease, oil and transmission fluid stained his navy work pants and the once-tan leather of his boots, but none of that was what she seemed to be seeing. "At least five years. I wasn't gone long."

Her gaze came up, her curiosity drawing her blond brows together. "I thought you were off to see the world and make your fortune."

He shrugged, tapped his toe against her calf again. "I did some sightseeing, took on some odd jobs to keep afloat. Didn't take me long to realize home is where the heart is, I guess you could say."

He expected her to question his possession of one. A heart. Instead she seemed to close up a bit, her voice taking on a hint of bitterness as she said, "It's good to know it wasn't broken."

He huffed. What? She expected him to admit how hurt he'd been? That he'd spent those months in Australia and New Zealand working her out of his system? They'd never had a real relationship. They'd had lust. And heat. And the sort of sex a man never forgot.

But none of that had anything to do with his heart.

The fluorescent light overhead flickered, reflecting off the lounge's big windows that looked out over the showroom floor. "I think that's why we worked so well in bed. We're both unbreakable."

The look she gave him was a silent touché, and it set them on a more even footing. Neither had been fair with the other. But they'd both grown up, and the past was in the past—even if he was suddenly having a hard time keeping it there.

He shifted forward in his seat, braced his elbows on his knees and laced his hands between. This close, he could smell her, that subtle scent of a spicy sort of flower, the same as it had always been, reminding him how often he'd turned and expected to find her there since he'd last seen her.

He'd hated himself for that weakness. "I've got

work to do, Milla. I need to get back. So can we get to the point here?"

She smoothed her palms over the straight black skirt she wore. It made her legs look paler than they were. "I wanted to ask you for a favor."

A favor? "A favor."

A hesitant smile crossed her face. "It seemed like a good idea at the time."

"And what time was that?"

"When I saw your card."

"But now that you've seen me, it doesn't?"

More smoothing. Some toying and plucking at her hem. "It's not that."

"Then what?" God help him, he really wanted to know. He reached for her fingers. They were cool and small and so…fragile in his. It was hard to keep his voice steady. "What is it, Milla?"

She raised her gaze to meet his. "Seeing you again…it's brought back so many things… I don't know what I was thinking, coming here."

The fact that he was more interested in what she was thinking now was as telling as deciding they could get back to what she *had* been thinking later. Why had he assumed that he'd see her again? "What's the favor?"

"I need a date for tomorrow night."

"A *date?*" He hadn't seen her for six years and she'd come to ask him for a date?

"Actually, for tomorrow and the next two Friday nights," she added, rushing on. "It's work-related. I do club reviews for a relationship Web site."

"Club reviews," he said, his echo of her words sounding ridiculously inane. He was stuck processing the reality of Milla Page asking him out on a date.

"I know, I know." She pulled her fingers free and got to her feet, grabbing her purse and heading for the door before he could stop her. "I don't know what I'm doing here. I shouldn't have come."

Neither did he, but he'd bet the farm it had nothing to do with needing a date for work. "What time do you want me to pick you up?"

She stopped, turned, kept her gaze locked on his as he stood to tower above her. "You don't have to do this, Rennie. I'll find someone else."

"You came to me for a reason, Milla." When she started to interrupt, he held up one hand. "I'll be damned if I know what it is, but we'll figure it out later. Tell me what time and where to find you."

Her fingers were trembling when she dug into her purse for a pen and her card. She printed an address on the back. "That's where I live. The other side is work. Call me at six?" When he nodded, she went on. "My cell, office and home numbers are all there."

"And where are we going?" He studied the card. "So I'll know what to wear."

"Oh, it's a club in the Presidio. Test Flight. The dress is trendy casual."

"I'll see what I've got in my closet." She hesitated, as if wanting to respond to what he'd said. He saved her the hassle of asking what he was going to wear. "Don't worry, Milla. I know how to clean up."

"I wasn't worried about that." She reached up to push away loose strands of hair. "I just hadn't thought that I might be putting you out. If you have other plans—"

"If I had other plans, I'd be keeping them," he said, glad he didn't have to test that theory. "I'll call you tomorrow at six."

She nodded, turned and vanished from his showroom the same way she'd vanished from his life.

He waited for the hurt to return, for numbness to follow. Instead he felt the same adrenaline rush he got when test-driving one of his show's new rides.

And right then he knew he was in trouble. He wouldn't know how deeply until tomorrow night, a thought that sent him slamming out of the showroom to bury himself in work.

HECTOR PRIETO STOOD in the doorway of the shop office and watched Rennie drop back to the creeper and shove himself beneath the panel van.

Whatever had happened between the boss and the stick chick couldn't have gone down too good. Ren might as well have dragged a storm cloud back with him into the shop.

Gloom and doom. That's what Hector was feeling. And that was no way to be working when they had so much to do.

His own team of mechanics was in pretty good shape, working to tear down Ren's Studebaker for a show that would run toward the end of the season. But that didn't mean anyone could slack off.

"Yo, Angie."

Behind him, Angie Soon straightened from where she'd been digging through the invoices in Ren's file cabinet. "I am busy here, Hector. I am not at your beck and call."

Women. Cripes. Thirty years old, and he still didn't understand them. Hector glanced at her over his shoulder. "I'm not becking or calling. I wanna know what went down with Ren and the woman who came to see him. Did they have a fight or something?"

"What did I just say, Hector? I've been working." Angie straightened, gestured with both hands, her bright pink nails flashing. "That phone up front doesn't stop ringing just because Rennie decides to get into it with some woman who drops in out of the blue."

"Humph." Hector stepped back into the office. "They got into it, huh? What happened?"

Angie bent over to dig through the files again, inadvertently giving Hector an eyeful. Her blouse gaped open as she flipped through the folders, and he didn't even think about looking away.

Her breasts were tight and small, covered by a plain pink bra, the skin of her stomach smooth and white beneath. He found his palms itching, and he curled his fingers into them, his mouth dry, his blood hot.

He'd never thought about Angie like that before…

"I don't know exactly," she finally said, pulling out one file folder and flipping through the contents, strands of black hair falling into her face. "They were quiet, but neither one could sit still."

He crossed to the corner and pulled a tiny paper cup from the water cooler dispenser. "Where were they?"

"In the customer lounge. I could only see them through the glass. Rennie had that look on his face. That one where you can tell he's got something on his mind."

"Right. The one where he's not going to talk about whatever it is until he figures it out for himself." Hector downed the water, crumpled the cup and threw it away. "You think she's an ex or something?"

Angie shrugged, returning the folder and digging into another. "She could have been. Or she could have been a bill collector. Whoever she was, they definitely weren't having fun reliving old times."

Hector found himself smiling. Not so much at the idea of Rennie in trouble with a woman, but at Angie. Just at Angie. And just because. "Ren's back at work, so I guess there's no need to be worrying about it."

Clutching to her chest the folder she'd come for, Angie slammed the drawer with the swing of her hip. "I'm not worrying over anything but getting these missing receipts to the accountant. If you're worrying, then you obviously have too much free time."

He leaned against the doorjamb, crossed his arms over his chest, arched a brow. "Maybe I do. Maybe you could help me fill it up."

She stared at him for several long seconds, strands of hair catching on the folder she held. Her dark eyes were narrow and made up in colors of purple and blue to match her blouse. She kept her lips pressed together, and wore no lipstick.

For some reason her lips being bare like that made it easier for him to see when she started to go mad. "What exactly is it you're saying, Hector? And be very clear so I don't start thinking you meant something you didn't."

Cripes and double cripes. But since he was already in for a pound… "Tomorrow night. You want to grab a burger?"

"A burger?"

A burger and a beer would be better for a night with Rennie and Jin. "We could go for shrimp. Or steaks. Whatever you like."

"I like lasagna."

"Italian's good. You have a favorite place?"

She nodded. "I do. Thank you for asking."

"Okay, then," he said, pushing off the door. "I'll pick you up at seven-thirty."

She walked toward him, walked past him, walked out into the shop. "Don't be late. And don't honk. Come to the door. If you don't, you'll have to explain to my mamma that you are not disrespecting me."

"You still live with your mamma?"

She stopped and swung around, one hand going to her waist. "I take care of her. I support her. Do you have a problem with that?"

Hector shook his head quickly. He knew more than enough about supporting his own family, the sacrifices it took, how nothing about it was easy. He'd just never thought of Angie that way. Living like he did…

He'd just thought of her as the girl who answered

Bergen's phones. Not as a girl who might understand his life. "No problem. I was just asking, that's all."

Her cute little nose came up in the air. "Okay, then. Tomorrow night. Seven-thirty."

"On the dot," he assured her, thinking he really needed to stop looking down girls' blouses before he did something more stupid than inviting one out to eat.

UNBREAKABLE.

She couldn't believe he'd called her unbreakable. After all they'd shared and all they'd been through, did he really not know her at all?

Milla stood at the window of her office, staring at the afternoon traffic ten stories below, her late lunch spread out on the desk behind her.

She'd left Bergen Motors and driven for an hour before realizing she'd done nothing but go nowhere. She didn't like that about herself. The way she so easily drifted, searching, unsatisfied. It was a state with which she'd become too emotionally intimate the last few years.

When she'd finally arrived back downtown, she'd stopped at the deli on the corner for a sandwich, realizing she hadn't eaten since the night before. But thinking of Rennie made it impossible to think of anything else, no matter all the things on her mind.

Food, work, the new shoes that pinched her feet and she needed to return, the book in her drawer she'd wanted to finish at lunch, deciding on a dress for tomorrow night, the fact that Natalie would be stopping by any minute for a blow-by-blow of Milla's morning excursion—

"How'd it go?"

Smiling at the confirmation of her uncanny sixth sense, Milla turned, hoping the tracks of her tears had dried. She pulled in a shuddering breath. "I have a date, if that's what you're asking."

"That's good, and Joan will be pleased, but that's not what I'm asking." Natalie closed Milla's office door, her silk jacket swinging around her hips, her gaze sharp and demanding. "What happened with your Mr. Bergen?"

Hugging herself tightly, Milla avoided her friend's eyes that saw too much, staring at her soggy sandwich instead. "Not much, actually. We talked for less than ten minutes."

Gripping the back of the gold-and-blue paisley visitor's chair, Natalie leaned forward. "Talked? About?"

"Honestly? Nothing. Absolutely nothing." Milla dropped into her own chair, pulled a pickle from her sandwich and popped it into her mouth.

"So, what then? You compared notes on the weather? The state of the union? Old times?"

"He said, 'What're you doing here?' I said, 'I don't know.' He said, 'What took you so long to look me up?' I said, 'I don't know, but would you like to go out tomorrow?' He said, 'Sure, I'll see you then.'" She chomped on a tomato slice. "And that was it. Like I said. Ten minutes and absolutely nothing."

Natalie stepped back and frowned. "But he said he'd go out with you."

Milla nodded.

"And you'll talk more then?"

She couldn't even measure the level of dread in her stomach. "If not, it will be an uncomfortably dull date."

"Then it is a date?"

All she knew was what she'd told Rennie. "A work date. Not a hot and heavy night on the town."

"Hmm."

"What's that supposed to mean?" Milla asked as Natalie finally circled the guest chair and sat.

"It's not supposed to mean anything. I was just thinking."

"About?" Milla pinched off a triangle of cheese.

"How two people with the history you and Rennie Bergen share could get anything out of your systems in ten minutes and by saying nothing."

Another triangle of cheese. Another pickle slice. She tasted none of it. "Who said we had anything to work out of our systems?"

"I did, but no one has to say it to make it so. Just like no one has to say there's been an earthquake when the cracks in the wall tell the tale."

Milla chuckled beneath her breath, deciding the sound was a bit too hysterical for comfort. "Are you saying I'm cracked?"

Natalie's fingernails rat-tatted against the chair's maple arms. "I'm saying you haven't been whole since the last time you saw Rennie Bergen."

"That's ridiculous," Milla said, unable to swallow.

"Is it?" Natalie's dark brows winged upward. "I

may not have known you then, but I know you now. And I've been waiting a long time for you to make your way back from wherever it was that he left you.".

"He didn't leave me anywhere," Milla grumbled.

"Don't interrupt." Natalie held up one elegant finger. "You haven't wanted to face the impact Rennie Bergen had on your life. I figured that first you had to reach your breaking point. Maybe this was it."

Milla remained silent and continued to pick at her sandwich. It was easier to pick at the veggies, cheese and bread than her life. "Rennie said I was unbreakable."

Natalie, always so poised, actually squeaked. "What?"

"Unbreakable." Milla shook her head because she couldn't think of anything else to do. "He said we both were."

"And you believed him?"

She didn't know what to believe. To tell the truth, as often as she thought about Rennie Bergen, she'd never expected to see him again.

They'd come from different worlds, lived different lives. Nothing about their time together had been normal. Even the first time they'd met, what they'd done, nothing about it had been right.

It had all been so very wrong....

3

Nine years ago…

MILLA SAT ON THE end of the bed in Derek's dorm, thumbing through his psych text and listening to Nirvana while waiting for him to get back.

An hour ago they'd finished off his roommate's six-pack, and Derek had decided to replace it tonight. Rennie got in from work at ten and would be looking to unwind. Finding the minifridge empty would make him one unhappy camper.

But it was ten, and Derek was still gone, and Milla wasn't sure whether to keep waiting and risk his roommate getting pissed or to cut out for home. It wasn't like she was afraid of Rennie blowing a gasket over them drinking his beer. Really, what could he do?

But Derek insisting they make things right before Rennie got home did make her uneasy. Especially when she took into consideration everything else her boyfriend had told her about Rennie Bergen. About where he'd come from, the way his life was the flip side of theirs.

How he was so hard to read, so quiet. How he kept himself apart from the other guys when they'd all go out to party or to basketball games. How, when he did laugh, his sense of humor was wicked, almost cruel, as if he never had anything nice to say. As if he hated the world around him.

When she combined all of that with the fact that Derek never felt the need to cover his own ass… She swallowed hard, wishing he would hurry up. She didn't know why she hadn't told him earlier that she needed to go home. She had a ton of research to do before she could finish her paper.

Just then, she heard his key in the lock. Her fingers curled into the bedspread and she scooted forward, closing up his book and ready to call it a night. Only it wasn't her boyfriend that walked through the door.

It was Rennie Bergen.

Her heart jumped into her throat and lodged there, making it impossible to breathe without feeling as if her chest were going to explode. God, why hadn't she left earlier? Why had she come here at all? How was she going to get out of here now without him thinking she was running away?

He was taller than Derek by a couple of inches, his shoulders broader, the look in his eyes older than any of the guys she hung out with. She knew he'd just had a birthday and turned twenty. Derek had thrown him a kegger last weekend, but she'd been too sick with cramps to go.

Now she wished she'd made it so this wouldn't be

their first meeting, here in this very small room while she was sitting alone on a bed. Still, she met Rennie's surprised gaze head-on, trying to smile—and to find something intelligent to say.

"Hi." She gave a weak wave with one hand. "I'm Milla."

Rennie nodded, glanced around the room. "Where's Derek?"

His voice was gruff and she felt her face flush as his gaze came swiftly back to hers. She gestured again just as uselessly as before. "He went to the store. He should be back any minute."

Rennie didn't acknowledge her answer, but flung his duffel bag onto his bed where it bounced. He then crossed to the minifridge that sat between his and Derek's desks, his strides long, the muscles beneath the fabric of his jeans and T-shirt impossible to ignore. He was built way better than Derek…everywhere.

It was after he'd pulled open the fridge, and had been staring silently into the empty interior for what seemed like forever that Milla found her full voice. "Derek went to get beer. For you. To replace what we drank."

He closed the fridge door softly. Milla had expected to hear it slam. She watched as he straightened and turned toward her again. The deeply slashed V of his brows and the way his throat was working didn't exactly frighten her, but did set her even further on edge.

And a big part of that, she feared, was a restlessness caused by the way he looked.

And the way he was looking at her.

His eyes were brown, dark and smoky. Like coffee with rising steam. He had a faint shadow along his chin and jaw, as if he hadn't shaved in a couple of days. She wanted to touch it. It intrigued her. Derek hardly had to shave at all.

Rennie's lips were full, both brackets on either side of his mouth deep. He looked like he worried too much, or didn't smile often enough. He looked like the grooves had set in to stay. And that intrigued her even more.

She didn't think any guy had ever made her tingle the way she was by doing nothing more than staring into her eyes. It was the way she'd felt when Dennis Quaid kissed Ellen Barkin in *The Big Easy*. The way she'd felt watching them in bed, aching to feel that same breathless sort of desire.

Sure, she got excited when making out with Derek, and the sex was okay. But she'd never wanted to take off her clothes because of the look in his eyes. Rennie Bergen made her want to get naked.

She groaned beneath her breath. She was in so much trouble here.

"What's wrong?" he asked, his voice as coarse as the rest of him.

Was that what it was? He wasn't a gorgeous jock like Derek was? He was rough, and maybe a little bit dangerous because so much about him was unknown? Plus he was older. She shrugged. "Just wondering what's taking Derek so long."

He moved toward her, stopping to lean against the end of Derek's desk, facing the bed where she sat. His hands were so big where they curled over the edge on either side of his hips. "There's a wreck blocking the entrance gate to the dorm complex."

Her heart fluttered. "Derek?"

Rennie shook his head. "Two compact imports. And both the wrong color."

Derek's classic Corvette was candy-apple red. She breathed easier, then she frowned. "How did you get in? If the entrance is blocked?"

Rennie canted his head toward the door. "A buddy dropped me off about a mile back. I hoofed it."

That's right. He'd totaled his car a month ago and was on foot until he got another. And then she remembered more. The Bergen's family-owned a car lot. "You can't get a loaner from your dad? Until you find something you want?"

"I have found something I want," he told her, crossing one ankle over the other and drawing her attention again to the fit of his jeans, to his legs that were muscled and long, to his hips that were narrow and lean.

God, where was Derek? "But no loaner in the meantime?"

He shook his head, his gaze sharp and piercing as he stared down to where she was sitting not three feet away. On the bed. Just like in *The Big Easy*. "I'd rather work for what I want. Make it mean something."

Were they still talking about cars? Or was he slamming Derek for having so many things handed to him?

And why was she suddenly so aware of his size? Or hers that was half of his?

"Well, sure," she said, twisting the silver pinky ring she wore. A gift from Derek. One the allowance his parents gave him had paid for. "But why not take the help in the meantime? Wouldn't it make your life easier? Give you more time to study and all?"

His expression hardened. "I don't mind walking."

Now he was just making her mad. "I don't mind walking, either. But I don't turn down help just to make a point."

He uncrossed his ankles, slowly pushed off the edge of the desk to stand straight. "You think I'm on foot because I'm making a point?"

Right now, she didn't know what to think. But she did know that she'd hit a nerve, so all she did was shrug. "Honestly, I have no idea."

"Then I'll tell you," he said harshly. "My insurance doesn't cover a loaner. I couldn't afford the policy if it did."

Oh. Now she felt bad. "So, get a loaner from your dad."

"My dad is the one who taught me to work for what I want," he said, shoving his hands deep in his pockets.

Meaning, his dad wouldn't *give* him a thing. God, she was so thick sometimes. "Well, then I guess working's what you've gotta do, huh?"

It took a few seconds, but he seemed to relax, blowing out a slow breath. He pulled his hands free from his pockets and shoved them back over his hair, which looked wet, as if he'd just washed it.

Even the grooves on either side of his mouth softened, though they didn't disappear. "Yeah. For now."

She thought for a minute; since they were all business majors here…

"If you need tutoring…or help…" She paused, not certain what he might need, what she could offer, if anything useful at all. "Or if you need a car, you can borrow mine. I use it, but sometimes it sits for days."

His frown returned. "You got a good battery?"

She barely stopped herself from rolling her eyes. "I wouldn't offer the car if I didn't."

"No, I mean…" He gestured with one hand. "If you let it sit too long, a couple of months or so, your battery can go bad."

"Oh." She'd thought he was being critical when what he was was actually concerned. Didn't say much for her perceptiveness that she couldn't tell the difference. "Thanks. But I do use it at least once a week."

He nodded. "You'll be fine then. But Derek's probably told you that."

Actually, Derek hadn't told her a thing. "The only car Derek cares about is his own."

Rennie studied her face for a moment, his expression not quite a frown, but one of confusion. As if what she'd said didn't make sense. "Thanks. For the offer. If I do use it, I'll run it by the shop and make sure it's in good shape."

Wow. That wasn't what she'd expected at all. "Why would you do that?"

"Because that's another thing my dad taught me to do."

"Take care of cars?"

"Well, yeah. But I was talking about taking care of people."

"You're lucky then," she said, looking down at her hands and wishing Derek would hurry up and get back. Her pulse was racing too hard, her heart softening. "A lot of parents teach their kids that everything is easily solved with money."

He snorted. "You mean it's not?"

She smiled, tugged on her pinky ring. "It could be, I suppose, but it means more if you have to work for it, right?"

This time he laughed, chuckled really, the sound deep and full and honest. "I'm a prick. I admit it."

"I wouldn't say that," she said, a strange thrill spinning in the pit of her stomach, her voice dropping as she added, "I wouldn't say that at all."

The seconds that followed ticked by in silence, and Milla wished she could take back her careless words. She was playing with a fire that she sensed could get her burned—and burned badly. Yet she didn't understand why.

She was happy enough with Derek. She didn't need the sort of complications a guy like Rennie Bergen would bring to her life. But she couldn't stop herself from playing with the fire that had started the minute they'd found themselves alone.

She wanted to know if it was her, or if it was Rennie making her feel this way. She wanted to know if this antsy restlessness, this itchy anticipation, was what she should be feeling for Derek.

Finally, Rennie moved, clearing his throat as he walked toward the bed. "If not a prick, then what?"

Misunderstood, she wanted to say. *Hard to read. Impossible to figure out.* Instead she got up and headed for the door. "I need to go. Tell Derek I waited as long as I could. I've got a psych paper coming due, and I need to get back to it."

"Wait," he called just as her hand found the doorknob. "Milla, wait."

Hearing him say her name… She bowed her head, dropped her chin to her chest, her forehead against the door. She didn't say a word. Just closed her eyes, held her breath and waited for what she'd been wanting so terribly since he'd walked into the room.

She felt him when he drew close. Felt his shadow. Felt his heat. She also felt so small, so fragile…and so in the wrong.

She and Derek were exclusive. That meant being faithful. Not cheating. Resisting the temptation of lust. But, oh, it was so hard to do when her heart was beating as if it had finally found a reason to do so, as if it never wanted to stop.

"Turn around," Rennie said softly, and without a second thought she did, her hands coming up between them to push him away, to keep their bodies apart. He took hold of her wrists and pinned them to the door on either side of her head.

"We can't do this," she argued, looking no higher than the dip in his throat where his pulse hammered and his veins popped. "It's not fair to Derek."

"This doesn't have anything to do with Derek," Rennie said, his voice a deep, throaty growl. "This is about you and me."

"There is no you and me." She swallowed hard, hating herself for not pulling away, for being too weak to walk out like she should.

Her chest heaved as she waited, her hardened nipples drawing Rennie's gaze to her bright-red T-shirt. "We're the only ones here."

"Rennie, please," she found herself saying, found herself whimpering, not knowing if she was begging him to stop or to go on.

Her eyes were closed so she didn't see him lower his head. She didn't see the way he parted his lips, or the way his nostrils flared. She didn't see the downward sweep of his lashes that hid the glimmer of emotion in his eyes.

But she imagined it all. And then his mouth was on hers, his body dipping to align with hers, his tongue pushing forward to find hers and play.

She opened her mouth because she had to. And she didn't even pretend to struggle against his hold.

It was a beautiful kiss, and she wanted to cry. He was tender, the press of his lips firm, yet yielding, the stroke of his tongue like being licked by a flame.

She shuddered and kissed him, giving up the parts of herself she was used to holding back, understanding nothing of the reason for what or why she did.

All she knew was that Rennie Bergen filled the very need he'd brought into existence. A need from which she would never be able to kiss herself free.

It was too much, more than she knew what to do with, more than she was ready for. And it was a very big more she was afraid she couldn't live without.

Finally she pulled her mouth from his, tugged loose her hands and ducked out from under his body. "I've got to go. I've got to go."

He let her. He stepped out of the way, allowed her to open the door, didn't stop her from scurrying down the hall. But he did laugh.

She heard it echo behind her. The sound was dry and bitter, as if she'd proved him right. She didn't have it in her to stay and work for what she wanted.

Like her kind did, she was taking the easy way out.

WHAT IN THE HELL was a girl like Milla Page doing with a guy like Derek Randall? Rennie liked Derek well enough, but the other guy had made it clear that he was in school to party, and Milla was not a party girl. Until tonight, Rennie hadn't known that. He hadn't known it at all.

If he were judging her by her looks alone and the fact that she came from money…yeah, he could see her squeaking by in school and having a hell of a good time in the process. She had the face, the body, the perfect tits and ass. But that was such a small part of who she was.

And he wished he hadn't discovered the truth. That she was nice, thoughtful, funny and smart. Because while Rennie didn't have a problem with partying, he was here for the degree. And now he was going to have a hard time thinking of Milla as Derek's—and keeping his mind on school.

He'd seen her with Derek but always at a distance, and hadn't talked to her until tonight. She wasn't anything like what he'd expected. A girl dating Derek Randall, the All-American party-boy jock, had to be as shallow and self-absorbed as he was. Milla was anything but. Meaning the best thing Rennie could've done was stay out of her way.

Instead he'd done the worst.

He shook his head, whipped off his T-shirt and headed for the shower. He'd cleaned up at work, but didn't want to be here when his roommate got back. He didn't want to have to explain where Milla had gone, why she had left.

But he didn't have anywhere to go, or the money to get him there if he did. Hiding out in the shower made him a prick, but it was better than going off on Derek for no reason but envy.

And it was a hell of a lot better than betraying Milla by throwing what they'd done into her boyfriend's face.

Besides, the steam and the hot water and the being alone would give him time to think. He needed a workable plan.

One that would guarantee he won Milla Page for himself.

RENNIE SHOOK OFF the past, returned to the present and reached for his cell, wondering what had possessed him to recall the first time he'd talked to Milla. The first time he'd kissed her. The first time he'd realized how perfectly they fit.

Oh, the places they'd gone from there…

And why was he wasting time with a trip down memory lane when he had the whole night ahead to figure out what Milla really wanted? Not to mention get a handle on why he seemed to be so accommodating considering their past.

He'd programmed her numbers yesterday and now hit speed dial while he drove toward the city, figuring no matter where she was, her cell would be the quickest way to reach her.

"Milla," she said after two rings.

"Rennie," he replied just as succinctly, realizing for the first time how little they'd ever needed to say to one another, how busy they'd been touching and feeling and teasing, all of it without words.

"Hey. Oh, it's six. God, this day has been crazy."

The first jolts of unease rippled through him. "That sounds like you're thinking of canceling on me."

"Oh, no, no." She laughed, a nervous, breathy sound. "Going out is part of the job. I can't cancel."

Right. He'd managed to forget that for her this was about work. It wasn't about him. So, why in the hell was he nearly tripping over himself to help her? "Where are you?"

"I'm still at the office, but I was just getting ready to head home." He heard the clatter of her keyboard. "I've got to shower and change, but it shouldn't take too long. If you don't mind waiting, you could meet me there? Or if you've got anything you need to do, you could swing by around seven-thirty?"

He found himself smiling and stopped. "I don't have anything to do, so I'll see you in twenty."

"Great," she said, and reminded him of her address before she disconnected the phone.

Not too shabby, he mused as he headed that way. Who knew dating for a living paid so well…unless she was living above her means or spending her inheritance, still of the mind-set that those who *had* were somehow more well thought of than those who *had not*.

Then again, he wasn't sure she'd ever embraced that ideal as fully as the rest of the moneyed crowd she'd run with. He'd been the lone exception. What had drawn them together came from a visceral, baser place inside both of them and had nothing to do with material things. Their infatuation had been…unexplainable.

All these years later—and for no reason he could fathom—he was hoping to finally solve the puzzle. This time with her might have fallen into his lap, but it still presented the perfect occasion to work Milla Page from his system for good.

4

"MAKE YOURSELF AT HOME," Milla said, tossing her purse and key ring on top of a wooden secretary in the entryway and setting her cell in a charger there.

"There's a bar in the kitchen and a freezer full of ice. There's also coffee in the basket next to the coffee-maker. The living room's off the kitchen, and I figure you can find the TV. Give me thirty minutes, okay?"

"No rush," Rennie replied, as she did just that— rushed down the center hallway of her third floor flat in the Inner Richmond Victorian and out of his sight.

Yeah. So far, so bad, he mused with no small amount of self-directed sarcasm. It was always a good sign when a date ran away.

He'd arrived only moments behind her, following her from where they'd parked in the street up the three flights of stairs to her door.

She'd smiled at seeing him, but then avoided his gaze, tossing talk of the weather over her shoulder while they'd climbed.

For all the attention she paid him, he might as well have been a stranger—one with whom she had no history, one to whom she had nothing to say. One who had never meant anything to her, who had never been a part of her life.

It was when she'd dropped her keys while unlocking the door that he'd admitted he wasn't being fair. In fact, he was being the same prick he'd been too much of the time while in school.

He was older. He should be wiser. And he was—at least wise enough to realize she was nervous.

First it had been the fumbling with the keys, then the mile-a-minute speech, then the flight to her bedroom. Nerves weren't exactly what he associated with the Milla Page he'd spent four years getting to know, and he couldn't help but be curious at the change.

He was also surprised that she'd left him alone. Doing so hinted at a level of trust he wasn't sure he deserved. Taking advantage never crossed his mind, but she had given him free run of the place.

And accepting her unspoken offer might give him an insight, a hint of why she'd come to see him…something he could latch on to that made sense.

Because finding himself in the entryway to her house all these years later didn't make any sense at all.

He headed for the back of the flat and the kitchen. Nursing one drink now couldn't help but ease some of the tension he was feeling. Coffee on the other hand might possibly send his blood pressure rocketing before the night even got off the ground.

He found a glass on the bar set up at the end of the

kitchen counter, found ice in the freezer, went back for a splash of Scotch and wondered why everything about Milla's place was so colorless and cold.

Her kitchen was as white as everything else he'd seen so far, the only color break, the stainless steel appliances. The countertops were a white marble with a thin gray vein. The floor was similarly tiled.

Even the items she had sitting out—the coffee-maker, the canister set, the mugs hanging on a rack—lacked any hint of color. Rennie frowned, sipped his drink, moved into the living room toward the TV.

There wasn't anything he wanted to watch, but at least the noise would give life to the room that made him think of bones bleached to death silently by the sun. This absence of color, of energy, of…soul wasn't right. It wasn't Milla.

Remote in one hand, drink in the other, he stood in front of the television and flipped through the channels without taking in any of the flickering scenes.

Milla had been vibrant, passionate. She'd dressed in bright colors. Reds, purples, hot orange. He'd never seen her wearing anything like the black skirt and pale yellow blouse she'd worn yesterday, or the similarly dull combination of pink and navy today.

Then he'd chalked it up to being the middle of a workday and her obvious business attire. Now that he'd seen what he had of her home, he wondered if it was something deeper, something more and telling.

He stopped flipping when he realized the station he'd stumbled on was showing a rerun of "Hell on

Wheels." It was the episode where his team had cut down an ambulance and turned it into a nitro-powered dragster.

And here he was sweating out the submersible idea. Then again, he pretty much sweated everything during the weeks it took to put together each one of the shows.

He didn't have to do it; even the conversions that bombed were a big hit with the viewers. The show's audience loved seeing the modification process and watching the crew put the tricked-out vehicles through their paces.

And Rennie, well, he loved getting his hands dirty taking care of his own, doing something that gave so much to so many people including fans, employees, family and friends.

In college, that had been Milla's role, the nurturer, the caretaker, the one who kept friendships from falling apart, who everyone looked to for answers.

He'd been the one living a dull and colorless workaholic existence. And look at them now, he thought as he sipped at his drink. It was role reversal in action.

When Milla had shown up so unexpectedly and propositioned him yesterday, he'd grabbed at the chance to finally work their past out of his system. Not that it was holding him back, or that he'd let those years eat at him all this time. Not that he hadn't moved on with his life.

The past was just there, and it didn't need to be. But now…now he wasn't so sure he was going to be able to walk away with a clear conscience without knowing more.

Because if there was anything he'd learned in the past twenty-four hours, it was that somewhere, somehow, Milla Page had been broken. And that was the most unexpected discovery he'd made since seeing her again.

"Sorry to take so long," she said, walking into the living room from the hall.

Nearly choking on his drink, Rennie clicked off the television, hoping he'd been fast enough to keep her from seeing his face or anything of the garage on the screen. He glanced at his watch—he'd been lost in thought for forty minutes—before he drained his glass and turned.

He found her struggling to tug the strap of her shoe up over her heel, found her wearing bright cherry-red. The color had always been one of his favorites. He wondered if she remembered, if she'd dressed with him in mind, if he was going to manage to get through the night without touching her.

When she straightened, her hair fell to frame her face, the shorter strands brushing her chin, the longer sweeping against her neck. In college, her hair had been soft and feathery. Now it was smooth, the ends stylishly flipping this way and that.

She looked great. She looked better than great. The light of which he'd only seen glimpses was back in her eyes. It set his blood to stirring, his fingers to itching, and his body began to warm.

He left the remote on top of the television and crossed the hardwood floor, returning his glass to the kitchen, turning to find she'd joined him. She'd grabbed her purse from the secretary and was now transferring the contents to a smaller bag.

He sat beside her at the table. The piece of furniture, not surprisingly, was painted white, the top inlaid with tiles the color of Ivory Snow. He watched as she sorted through her things. "Don't you get cold in here?"

She glanced up briefly. "Not really, why? Are you cold? I can turn up the heat."

"I'm not talking about the temperature. I'm talking about the igloo look you have going on." His encompassing gesture included both the kitchen and the living room beyond. "Or is white the new black or something?"

This time when she looked up, she seemed confused, but she did study her surroundings for several seconds before returning to the task of switching one purse for the other. "The place had just been painted when I bought it. The kitchen was newly tiled and the countertops were still being installed."

"Did it come furnished?"

She shook her head. "You can blame me for the dreary decor. I'm not here enough to really notice it, and it doesn't seem that important when I do. I've got too much else going on to worry about adding splashes of color."

He took that in, but didn't respond. He didn't know what to say. This was her home. Her supposed castle. He would think it would matter more than it did. "How long have you been living here?"

She closed up the purse he assumed she was carrying tonight and sat back, arms crossed, the fabric of her dress pulling tight over her small breasts. "It was a year in September."

Fourteen months without pictures. Without color. He wanted to know what kept her too busy to pay attention to her home. Then he changed his mind. He wasn't here to learn more about her. He was here to deal with what he already knew.

"Not a bad place," he said. "A little icy. A little plain."

"Some would say understated. Minimalist even." Her defensive posture tightened further.

"I'd say boring."

"What happened to icy and plain?" she asked, one brow lifting.

He shook his head. "Changed my mind."

"Spoke your mind, you mean," she said, and crossed her legs.

"Always have."

"I remember it well."

"Do you think that's why we fought so often?" He ran an index finger along the edge of the table's tiles, watching her eyes as they flashed. "Because I tend to say what's on my mind?"

She took several seconds to gather her thoughts, smoothing the hem of her dress as she answered. "I think we fought because we were up against more than either of us was able to deal with."

He snorted. "You mean, you cheating on your boyfriend with his roommate and me going behind Derek's back to do his girl?"

"Yes." Her gaze snapped to his. "That's what I mean. And when you put it like that—"

"How else should I put it, Milla?" he interrupted to ask. "Isn't that exactly what happened?"

She glanced down at her hem again, glanced back. "Like I said, I don't think either of us knew how to deal with it then. I'm beginning to wonder if we'll ever be able to. Or if we'll be stuck with each other forever."

He sat there for several long moments. This was not at all how he'd expected this evening to go. He knew they'd have to deal with their history eventually. But to have it weigh them down first thing…

Even worse was realizing how much of what he'd once felt for her was still there. That he'd forgotten the sting of her betrayal at the end, or at least pushed it aside to make room for the memories of good times they'd had.

Still, he had to ask. "Do you want me to leave? To call this whole thing off?"

She shook her head, her eyes bright and curiously challenging, her words equally so. "I just want to know why six years later we can't get beyond snapping off each other's heads."

"That one's easy," he said, his voice gruff. "We're both wondering if the other is going to make the first move."

He hadn't come here to get physical, but it wasn't hard to understand that his mind would go there considering most of the time he'd spent with Milla they'd been naked together in bed.

He held her gaze as she watched him, studied him, took him in and dissected him, and he waited for her to spit him back out in chewed-up, ground-up pieces. But she didn't move.

She just sat there, her arms crossed, her purse on her lap, the ends of her blond hair cupping her face. The pulse beating at the base of her throat was the only sign he wasn't sitting at the table with a mannequin.

He had no idea what she was thinking, if the intense scrutiny she was subjecting him to was the beginning of the end of their reunion, or if she was considering some other move that would derail the hopes he had riding unexplainably high. When—and how—had he become so involved in the outcome of this night?

What finally gave her away and set his spine to tingling was the clingy fabric of her dress, and she knew it. A blush of color washed up her neck as her nipples grew hard, drawing his gaze. He was a man; he remembered her well, and his blood flowed hot.

Yet she continued to silently take his measure, as if deciding whether he was worth another minute of her time or if the past they shared would prevent them from being friends, much less lovers.

He started to get up, wrap his fingers around her slender wrist, lead her to the door and down the stairs and into the front seat of his car. She had a job to do, one critical enough to bring her back into his life, and this standoff was getting her nowhere.

It didn't matter that he'd meant what he'd said, he never should have said it. Never should have let on that he hadn't outgrown his tendency to be crass, or any of his back-alley, pricklike, down-and-dirty ways.

But she stopped him from doing any of that by sitting forward and placing her purse on the table. And then she got to her feet and took his breath away by saying, "I already made the first move. I came to see you."

He swallowed a groan, his body aching. "You don't want me to make the next one. Trust me on that."

"Why not?" She took a step closer, stared down. "I can see what you want, Rennie. It's in your eyes. You forget how well I know you."

This wasn't the Milla who'd come to the shop to see him. This wasn't the Milla with no color in her life. This was the Milla of old, the one who'd never walked out on him after that first kiss up against the door of his dorm.

"I haven't forgotten anything at all," he managed to get out.

"Then do it," she said, bracing her hands on his thighs above his knees and leaning forward to whisper into his ear. "Make the next move."

He could smell so many of his memories on her skin. He was caught by them, unable to separate the present from the past. She hovered above him, reminding him of the best years of his life. If pressed, he could number the days.

He knew every place they'd been together, remembered taking her in public, in private, in locations that weren't meant for lovers, not caring that they might get caught. And all of that came back to him now, rushing over him in a dark, heady wave of wanting and lust.

He covered her hands with his; her skin was warm beneath his palms as he looked into her eyes. "You better be sure this is what you want because I'm not here to play games. And I'm sure as hell not here for some twisted payback."

"Payback?"

"For the party. For Derek. For the other girls. Whatever you feel you have to get back at me for."

The shift in her expression was subtle, a window being closed, the subject deemed off limits. And that was fine with him. That night was one part of the past he'd just as soon forget—even though forgetting was a pansy-assed way out, and would never make anything right.

"That was a long time ago, Rennie," she said, knowing as well as he did that it had only been six years. "And this isn't a game."

That was all he needed to hear. He reached for the skirt of her dress, hiked it up around her hips and pulled her forward to straddle his thighs. She spread her legs and sat, scooting forward, wrapping her arms around his neck.

Her breasts grazed his chest, and her weight was nothing. He swore she hadn't put on a pound. Hurting her physically wasn't an issue; it never had been. That much he knew. But hurting her emotionally, damaging her, breaking her further...

He thought for a brief but clear moment about walking away. He even moved his hands to her waist to do so. She didn't give him time to do either, but came closer, pressing against him, her lips grazing the corner of his mouth.

"Why do you do this to me?" she whispered, touching her tongue to his lips. "It's not fair, you know. That I remember everything so vividly. That I've never been able to get enough."

Enough sex or enough of him? He wanted to know what she was looking for, but he didn't want to make the distinction between the two, to separate the obvious part of his body from the rest of who he was.

Besides, he was just as desperate to have her and wasn't thrilled with what that said about him. He should have moved beyond needing her this way, beyond feeling whole when he was with her.

"It's not too late. We can stop. We don't have to do this." The offer was weak, but he made it.

She shook her head. "I don't want to stop. I don't want to think. I just want to feel. God, Rennie, I need to feel."

Alarm bells went off, clang-boom-bang in his head. Colorless and cold and broken. And now this desperation. Something was wrong here. He didn't know what it was, needed to find out, to push her away, to make her talk goddammit, to tell him what the hell was going on.

But then he breathed her in, that spicy floral perfume, the sweet earthy scent of her arousal. He knew she'd be hot and slick if he touched her. Knew she'd fit around him with the same snug hold as his fist.

He groaned as his cock swelled, groaned again when she shifted to rub against his shaft. They had to get this out of the way, this lust, this living, breathing need for one another.

They needed to connect with where they'd come from, with what they'd been to each other in the past. If they didn't, the night would be a bust, the weekend garbage, and the regrets and might-have-beens more haunting than before.

And so he touched her, slipping his hands from her waist to her thighs and beneath her short hem. Her skin was warm where he'd expected cool, what with the way she was exposed and was wearing next to nothing and the strip of her panties was so damp.

She shuddered, rested her forehead against his, began to pant in soft puffs of breath when he captured her clit between his thumbs. He pinched and pressed, rolled and rubbed, feeling her moisture spread and her temperature rise.

"You like that?" His chest ached. He had to push out the words.

She nodded, brushing her chin to his cheek, her nose to the bone of his brow. "I'd like it better if you'd do something with my panties."

He took hold of the fabric and tore it. "Something like that?"

"Exactly like that."

She was naked in his hands, her sex and the downy soft hair so familiar. He pulled her dress higher and out of the way, then looked down and drank her in.

He wanted to eat her up, to suck her into his mouth, to tongue her until she came all over his face. His cock throbbed, and he ground his jaw against the need to feel her fingers wrapped around his shaft. He held her by the waist and hefted her onto the table, pulling off her shoes and placing her feet on his thighs.

She leaned back on her elbows, watching him, her lips parted, her eyes sparkling, the color in her face running high. He held her gaze, pushed her dress to her waist, got rid of the remnants of her panties, and bared her to the room.

The sharp, needy sigh she exhaled went through him like a shot when he should have known to expect it. Hell, how many times had he heard it in the past? How many times had just thinking about it sent him to the shower to unload?

Hearing it now… He groaned, feeling the noise like a hard knot of anger in his gut. He shouldn't be angry. He wasn't angry…but he was. With himself. Because he had never managed to shake her hold.

He wanted to take his time with her, to take her to bed and linger over her, to spend hours talking to her, touching her, loving her in all the ways he knew that she liked. And thinking that way did nothing to improve his mood because their time together had been a lie.

They had not been a couple. They'd betrayed a good friend. They'd never discussed a shared future, as if knowing their stolen moments could never be anything more. And so instead of taking his time, he grabbed her ankles and stood, pulling her hips to the edge of the table before he found a condom in his wallet and unzipped his pants.

She watched as he sheathed his erection. She groaned again when he grabbed the base of his shaft and stepped between the V of her legs. He used the head of his cock to spread her moisture and ease his way. He pushed forward slowly, and her eyes widened the deeper he slid.

When he hit bottom, he stopped, holding himself still, throbbing when she tightened her muscles and milked him. He hissed back a sharp breath, closed his eyes, gritted his teeth and tamped down the head of steam he had ready to blow.

And then he began to move, slowly, rhythmically, in then out, over and over again. He leaned forward, braced his palms on the table next to her hips. She hooked her knees over his elbows, giving him better access and more room to play.

He pressed against her, rubbed the thick base of his shaft to her clit. She gasped, arched her neck, and came up off the table. He ground harder, forced her down with his weight and the motion of his body, grunting with each thrust and nearly coming undone.

It was raw and savage sex, lacking anything resembling tenderness, the purist sort of wicked lust needing to be slaked. He was ruthless in using her, in giving their past life in the present. She lifted her hips to meet every stroke, and he pounded into her, his fingers curling against the tabletop, his thighs slamming the edge.

He came at her first cry of completion, shuddering, aching, spilling himself inside of her as she contracted around him, pulling him deep and pumping him dry. The intensity nearly killed him.

He dropped his weight from his palms to his elbows, doing all he could just to breathe and saving what remained of his energy. He'd need it later to kick his own ass for being his own worst enemy—and proving once and for all the very thing he hadn't wanted to know.

His past with Milla Page would haunt him for the rest of his life.

5

HECTOR STOOD on the stoop outside of Angie's front door, smoothing down his tie and straightening the sleeves of his dress shirt. It was yellow, and was one of only two that he owned.

He had the money to buy more, but clothes weren't so important as the other things he had to take care of. Like his family. Seeing that they had what they needed. Medicine. Clean water. Food. A roof over their heads since they refused to leave El Salvador. He hoped this one would be okay, and that Angie wasn't expecting him to be a big spender.

Already he was thinking that this probably hadn't been such a good idea, him and Angie, but with the way his asking her to dinner had come out of nowhere, he hadn't had a chance to talk himself out of opening his big mouth.

He should have looked before he leaped or whatever the saying was, and considered his head being shaved and his wearing a goatee and the tattoo on his neck showing above the collar of his shirt, and how Angie might not be comfortable with all of that away from the shop.

But he hadn't. He'd just known that he wanted to spend some time with her that wasn't all about the mess he made of Ren's paperwork she spent so much time sorting out.

Shoot, he kept his hair cut off because it was a whole lot cooler that way when welding out in the yard. The goatee kept him from feeling naked.

And the tattoo, well, that he didn't mind so much since it reminded him of a big mistake he'd made a long time ago that he wasn't ever going to make again.

He'd run with the wrong crowd. He'd been lucky to get out. But he had. Thanks to the Bergen family and how they took care of their own.

Things now were going really good, what with the show and all, and finally making the kind of money that was giving his family a better life. He couldn't see anyone having a problem with that.

Having a problem with the trouble he'd been in, the trouble he'd caused... Yeah, he could see getting bent out of shape if he had a daughter and some skeevy punk showed to pick her up at the door.

But he'd never told Angie about his past, even though anyone who saw it would know the meaning of the tattoo. He hadn't even told her much about his present, and had never asked her much about hers. Like he'd had no idea she still lived with her mamma.

They never talked about anything but work. And now he was wondering why she even wanted to go to dinner with him. They might have nothing in common, he wasn't a big catch, and really he wasn't feeling so hot anymore.

He backed down the stoop and had turned to go when he heard the door open behind him. And so he stopped, feeling like a huge jerk and scrambling for something to say.

Angie beat him to it. "Hector Prieto. If you leave now, do not think you will ever be welcome inside this house again."

He found himself grinning as he looked up to where she stood framed in the open doorway. How come he hadn't ever noticed that she was so pretty? Her hair was so black it was almost blue, and her skin was perfect, and her mouth…well, he loved how she didn't wear lipstick.

"I'm not leaving," he said, slow to climb the stairs. "I was going to get my jacket out of the truck."

"For my sake, or for my mamma's?"

He shrugged, caught red-handed. "Both?"

She crossed her arms and stared down at him where he stood on the next-to-the-top step. He couldn't tell what she was thinking. He didn't think he'd ever before seen the look she had on.

It was as though she was seeing him for the first time, or seeing him as a different person than the one who didn't have it in him to care about paperwork. He wondered how come the both of them had finally decided all of a sudden to open their eyes.

"You can come in if you want," she finally said, moving back enough for him to walk through the doorway.

She made it sound like he had a choice. "You don't think I should get my jacket first?"

"You don't have to. You look fine." She glanced over his shoulder. "And my mamma's not here anyway. She went to bingo with my aunt."

He'd gotten dressed up and nervous, and for no reason? For a second there he thought about getting mad, but then he didn't. It wasn't Angie's mamma making him nervous. Or Angie's mamma he'd dressed for.

"Are we still going out? For lasagna?" he asked, brushing past her and into the house. She smelled sweet and clean, and the house smelled like cinnamon and apples. His stomach growled.

Angie laughed. "It sounds like you might want dessert first. Mamma put in an apple crunch before she left. I just took it out of the oven."

Hector wasn't sure what to say. He'd come here ready to answer questions about himself, to prove that he was a good guy with a good heart, to show that he respected Angie. And now it was just the two of them here.

"There's vanilla ice cream. To go with the apple crunch."

He couldn't help it. He smiled. "Lead the way."

The house was small, the kitchen right off a living room filled with knickknacks on doilies and ceramic statues and dozens of candles in glass holders painted with religious scenes. He expected the kitchen to be just as cluttered…and he was right.

Canisters and teapots and spice jars took up every inch of counter space. But the table was clean, covered with a yellow plastic cloth. That's where the apple crisp sat cooling, and where Angie told him to sit.

"Mamma doesn't always go to Friday night bingo. But Auntie June didn't want to go by herself." Angie offered up the explanation while setting two bowls and two spoons on the table. She then shoveled a serving spoon into the bubbling hot dish. "Do you want coffee to drink? Or tea?"

He usually drank orange soda. She knew that because she ordered extra cases for the shop every week. "Whatever you have is fine. But is this okay? Eating the dessert? Maybe your mother made it for a special reason?"

"She made it for you."

He looked over to where Angie was reaching into the freezer for the ice cream, her blouse pulling away from her low-rise pants and showing off a strip of skin at her waist.

Hector swallowed hard. "What do you mean, she made it for me?"

"I told her I had company coming by. She felt bad about not being here, so she welcomed you the way she loves to do. With food."

He didn't know what to say to that. Or what to say when Angie brought him an orange soda after bringing over the ice cream and her own cup of tea.

He sat there while she scooped up the apples and the ice cream and spooned up extra juice to drizzle on top.

He had been on his own and taking care of himself for so many years that being waited on didn't come easy.

"There," she said, sitting beside him once she'd returned the ice cream to the freezer. "Dessert first."

He looked away from the smile on her face to his bowl, and picked up his spoon. "If I eat all of this now, I'm not sure I'll have room for lasagna."

Angie didn't seem to share his concern. "Sure you will. There's the best Italian place ten blocks over. We can walk and burn off all this sugar on the way."

"That works," he said, spooning up a bite and watching her dig in. She ate as though she hadn't seen food in days, and it made him laugh.

"What's so funny?" she asked, glancing over.

"Nothing," he said, smart enough not to go there.

"Don't tell me nothing, Hector. If you're going to laugh at me, you had better be ready to tell me why when I catch you."

He shrugged it off and looked back at his dessert, hoping she bought the show. He didn't want her to kick him out now. "I was trying to remember the last time I ate dessert first."

She didn't believe him. He could tell by how quiet she got. And by the way she grew still. "Are you sure you weren't thinking that I eat too much or too fast and am going to turn into a fat pig?"

He held his spoon over his bowl, both forearms against the edge of the table, waiting for her to look him in the eye. She finally did, and he didn't think he'd ever seen eyes so clear and so dark. "What I was thinking,

Ang, was that it's nice to see a girl who likes to eat and doesn't try to hide that she does."

This time she set down her spoon. "I don't try to hide anything, Hector. I am exactly who I am. I thought you might have noticed that by now. I thought that might be why you asked me to dinner."

He wasn't about to tell her how he'd come to the decision after looking down her blouse. And seeing how much effort she and her mother had made for him, he felt like a jerk for doing that.

And then he felt even worse because he wasn't sure how to respond. "If you want to know why, I can't tell you exactly. I guess it was something about the way you looked at me in the office."

"How did I look at you?" Her voice sounded as if she was about to go mad again.

He shrugged because he didn't want to tell her the truth. And he sure didn't want to talk about stuff like thoughts and feelings. "Like you were thinking of talking to Rennie about getting in someone else to do his paperwork."

"You asked me out to keep your job?"

Women. Cripes. He dropped his spoon into his empty bowl and leaned toward her. "I asked you out because I realized that I know who you are at work, but that's all. It's not right when you work together for three years not to know someone better."

"Oh," was all she said as she picked up both of their bowls and carried them to the sink. "Is there something specific you want to know about me? Like my favorite color, or whether or not I sleep with a night-light?"

He thought about seeing her bra and wondered if her favorite color was pink. "Knowing that stuff isn't knowing you. It takes time to get to know a person. Not a lot of facts."

"What are you saying, Hector? That you want to know me enough that you'll spend the time it takes to do that?"

Was that what he wanted? Spending that time? Knowing her? Letting her know him? Telling her about where he'd come from? The mistakes he'd made in his past?

He took a deep breath and sat back in the chair, putting the distance between them he needed to make up his mind. It didn't take him long. "Angie Soon, I've got all the time in the world."

She smiled, a big bright smile with lots of teeth showing. "That's good to hear. Because getting to know me might take you just that long."

WHAT IN THE WORLD was wrong with her? What had she been thinking? Or was the better question, had she been thinking at all? Milla fastened her seat belt and sat back after giving Rennie directions to the club. He responded with a nod and didn't say a word. She was equally speechless.

When she'd gone to see him yesterday morning after drawing his card from the boot, she'd been nervous. And not unexpectedly so. She hadn't seen or heard from him since the night of the graduation party that had changed both of their lives. Derek's, too.

But tonight, nerves had nothing to do with what she was feeling. Seeing him when he'd driven up and parked, when he'd stepped from the car looking like he carried the million he'd left home to make as pocket change, his long dark hair slicked back, his eyes sharp and focused on her...

She pulled in a deep breath along with Rennie's scent that she remembered so well. It had gotten to her earlier, that subtle hint of fresh air and sunshine and woodsy outdoors.

He'd been standing behind her as she'd fought to fit her key in her lock, and all she could think about was wanting him as much after all these years as she'd wanted him way back when.

She'd dropped her key ring, picked it up and opened the door, then rushed away to compose herself. A lot of good her composing had done. The tension between them had been unbearably tight, and the way they'd chosen to ease it...

God, he had to think she was desperate, wanting to pick up where their relationship had left off without any discussion of what had happened since, or what had happened then. Nothing could have been further from the truth, yet her actions pretty much called the truth a lie.

Her actions also made it hard to sit without squirming on the seat. Her sensitive skin had been rubbed raw, and no matter how uncomfortable she was, she couldn't shake the sensation of having Rennie inside of her. How could she have forgotten the perfect way he filled her, the perfect way that they fit?

"Are you okay?" he asked out of the blue, and she realized what she thought had been a silent groan had been anything but.

"I'm fine. Just…trying to recover my wits, my sanity, my professional game face."

He glanced over. "As long as you're not regretting anything."

Oh, she had all sorts of regrets. A mental diary full. "About what happened in the kitchen? No. I'm not. Nothing at all."

It sounded good anyway. Not particularly convincing, but…mature. Because that's what they were doing here, wasn't it? Proving to each other that they were no longer reckless college kids but responsible adults who were all grown up?

"That might not have been the smartest thing either of us has ever done," Rennie went on to say. "But if we get hung up on it now, it'll be hard to move forward."

Where did he think they were going? Besides out for drinks? "It was just sex, Rennie. Nothing to lose sleep over."

All grown up indeed. More like she was playing at saying all the right things. What *was* one supposed to say to an ex-lover who suddenly wasn't so ex?

"Right. Sex." He gave a sharp little laugh. "It was always about sex with us, wasn't it?"

Is that what he thought? Seriously? She shifted in

her seat, angling her body away from the door so she could face him, and found staring at his profile rather than into his eyes made this conversation easier to have.

"Actually," she said softly. "That's not how I remember it at all."

He looked over just long enough to set her on edge. "Name me a time we were together that we didn't have sex."

She couldn't, of course. That intimacy had meant everything then. "Okay, but that wasn't the only reason we were together."

"When were we *together*, Milla?" he asked harshly, glancing in the rearview mirror but not toward her. "I seem to remember you being with Derek and me being with no one."

No one? Maybe no one special or no one for any length of time. Maybe no one he considered exclusive. But he hadn't been alone. He'd always had someone with him the same way she'd always had Derek.

She wanted to shake him but settled for shaking her head. "You know what I mean."

He was silent as he waited at the next intersection for the stoplight to change. "Why don't you explain it to me? Just so I'm sure."

Hardheaded and arrogant. Just like he'd always been. "The time we spent together wasn't just about sex. You know that. We talked about our families—"

He cut her off immediately. "That's right. How is Daddy Warbucks Page? He let go of your trust fund yet? Send you out into the big bad world alone? Or is he still paying your way piecemeal?"

"As a matter of fact, he's not paying for anything at all. He hasn't been since I left school." *Since I broke things off with Derek,* she wanted to add, but stopped herself from rubbing any salt in the wound.

"Really," Rennie said, his tone mellowing, his interest rising. "What happened?"

She wasn't about to give him a sordid blow-by-blow. Not that he'd asked for the details. It was just that this truth was one she wasn't ready for Rennie to know. How from the very beginning her being with Derek had been less her choice and more her father's.

"He didn't get his way," she said, and left it at that.

But Rennie wanted more. "What didn't he get?"

"He lost out on a very profitable partnership." A truth that had many more layers.

"And he took it out on you?"

"It's…complicated," she said, staring out the windshield and into the night.

The idea of her mother giving up the life she'd lived for thirtysomething years? It had been easier for Milla to take what she needed to live reasonably well, and sign over the balance of the trust fund to her parents.

A part of her had thought her father would accept the offer, call a truce, and forgive her for letting him down and making public her sordid behavior. He'd done the first, but not the second or the third. "Families are like that."

"And it's none of my business. Sorry," Rennie

said. "I tend to be a pushy prick when I need to let things go."

He was right, and it was a trait she knew well—but not one she held against him. "It's just nothing I can explain without getting personal."

"Right. I forgot. Tonight's about business."

He was back to being bitter, and could she blame him? What with the way she let him into her body but wouldn't share less intimate parts of her life? She faced forward in her seat again, saying, "A lot's gone on since the last time I saw you. Not all of it's been good."

"Not all of it bad, I hope."

"Oh, God no. I didn't mean that. Except for a lot of stress at work the last few months, life's been hunky-dory."

Rennie snickered. "I can't believe you still say that."

She felt herself blush. "Honestly, I can't remember the last time I did."

"Blaming it on the company?"

"Hmm. I should, considering I've been off kilter since seeing you again."

"Is that what you're calling it now? Off kilter?"

"Why not?" It was better than thinking she was going insane with the way she couldn't get him out of her mind. "What should I call it?"

"I've always been a big fan of the truth myself. I'd say call it what it is."

"I'll stick with off kilter, thank you." She was not going to speak the word infatuated, or whatever it was he was digging for. "And since when are you a big fan of the truth? I seem to recall you spending nearly four years lying to the guy you roomed with freshman year."

"And I seem to recall you spending the same four years saying it was all about self-preservation. That if Derek had discovered what we were doing behind his back…"

Derek's family had been powerful enough to have easily made life hell for Rennie and Milla both. It was that power she'd wanted to avoid running up against— especially having witnessed her father fall prey. "It was. That doesn't make it any less of a lie."

"Face it, Milla. Neither one of us was a saint back then."

"I know."

"Have you talked to Derek since the party?"

She shook her head. She'd seen him at a few large charity functions. They hadn't spoken. It was enough to read of his success in the electronic newsletter his firm sent to stockholders, and that her father forwarded each month.

She really needed to learn to hit delete. "No. But then, I haven't kept up with anyone from school."

When Rennie remained silent, she cast a glance his way. "What about you?"

"What about me?"

"Friends? From school? Do you still see them?"

"Not from college, no. I work with a couple I went to high school with."

"Would I know them?" She had met one or two of

his friends when she'd stopped by his house on occasion with Derek.

"I doubt it."

She pushed. "Who?"

"Nosy."

"Just making conversation." It was easier to talk about his life, to keep him from digging into hers. "They work at your family's dealership?"

"Not exactly."

"What does that mean?"

He hesitated. "They work for me."

"But you work for your family. Or do you own the dealership now?"

He glanced over and glared. "What's with the twenty questions?"

"Isn't catching up what old friends do?" *Especially when one is trying not to reveal that at twenty-eight years old she still doesn't know who she is?*

"So now we're friends?"

"Fine. Just call it natural curiosity."

"I have a separate business," he said after a short pause.

"Which is?" she asked, pushing again.

"Rebuilding engines. Doing bodywork."

"An extension of what you grew up doing."

"You could say that."

She clucked her tongue teasingly. "And after all that talk of seeing the world and lining your pockets."

"I did some then. I'm still doing some now."

"Well, I guess that's all anyone can ask for," she finally said and, crisis averted, settled back in her seat.

Rennie pulled into a parking slot and shut off the engine. "I cannot believe that came out of your mouth."

She stiffened. "What do you mean?"

"The Milla I knew in college would never have settled—"

She rushed to deny his accusation. "I haven't settled—"

"She would never have thought doing *some* of anything was enough—"

"I don't think that. That's not what I meant—"

"You were a rock, Milla. Unbreakable. And now you're...broken. What happened?"

You happened, she wanted to say. No. She wanted to scream. *I fell in love with you. I couldn't have you. And you walked out of my life.*

She didn't like to think about how different her life might have been if she'd remembered all Rennie had taught her about being strong, instead of collapsing the minute he was no longer around.

"Settling...that's as bad as giving up," he went on to say. "And that's just not you."

"I haven't given up anything," she insisted. "And I haven't settled. I was just...making conversation."

"Forever the peacemaker. Keeping things from becoming awkward?" His laugh was so familiar, so cutting. "You were always good at that. Making sure everyone was always comfortable. That no one was hurt or left out."

God, she knew where this was going. To a place she didn't want to go.

"Remember the night of the concert? How you stuck with me instead of with Derek because you didn't want to leave me alone…"

6

Eight years ago...

"C'MON, MILLA. It'll be a blast."

"We won't have as much fun in the pit without you."

"Are you kidding? You'd rather stay here than see Brandon Boyd up close?"

Milla glanced from Becca to Risa to Steph, wishing she was in the mood to party with her friends because the four of them always had such a great time. "I'd rather see the whole *band* up close, but my head is killing me."

Steph dug into her minipack for a prescription bottle. "I've got meds."

"I took something before Derek picked me up," Milla said, waving off the offer. "I told him I was going to hang out on the lawn and listen from here."

"Milla, sheesh. Get real," Becca said with no small amount of sarcasm. "It doesn't matter how long you've been dating him. You don't need to be letting Derek off his leash."

It was hard not to roll her eyes when she knew Derek

as well as she did. His family was her second one. They'd known each other for years. It had been assumed by the Randalls and Pages alike that her and Derek dating in high school was the first step in a journey that would culminate after college in a country-club wedding no one would ever forget.

But she didn't explain that history to her friends. She just said, "I don't keep Derek on a leash."

"Well, you should," Steph put in, tugging at the hem of her T-shirt. "Especially since Donna Burkhardt just followed him into the pit. She's not exactly one to respect boundaries, if you know what I mean."

Becca snorted. "Knowing Donna, she'll throw her underwear at Derek instead of onto the stage."

Both of her friends were right, but Milla wasn't in the mood for their advice. She had too much else on her mind. "I told him to give my ticket away, but he wanted me to come. So I said I would, but was staying out of the pit. He said fine."

"That's crazy talk," Steph said. "I can't believe you'd let Derek out of your sight, not to mention stay up here by yourself."

"I won't be alone." She started to glance over her shoulder, but knew the move would be telling. "Rennie's here. Derek knows I'm okay."

Risa leaned in closer, kept her voice low. "Talk about needing a leash. I've heard some not so nice things about Rennie Bergen."

"Like what?" Milla asked, wondering what her friends had heard. If there were rumors about her and

Rennie. If someone knew that he'd kissed her last year. That she'd kissed him back. That they'd been unable to keep their hands off each other since…

"He's not anyone you want to be alone with, that much I know. Even in a venue as crowded as this one," Becca said, looking around at the thousands of concert-goers scattered across the lawn.

Milla's heart began to race. "What have you heard exactly?"

"The same things you have, no doubt." Becca gave a careless shrug. "He likes things rough. He's dangerous. He doesn't take no for an answer. And he's not particularly…couth."

"Yeah," Steph added before Milla could interrupt. "Donna Burkhardt should go after him and keep her paws off Derek. He's more her type."

"Donna isn't getting her paws on Derek," Milla said firmly. "And I haven't seen any of that in Rennie. Not that I'm any big Rennie Bergen expert, but he was Derek's roommate. He's always seemed nice enough."

Her girlfriends glanced at one another then back to her. Risa was the one who finally spoke. "Just because he spent a year living with Derek doesn't mean you can trust him. Haven't you heard neighbors of serial killers talk about what nice people they always were?"

Milla crossed her arms. "Rennie is not a serial killer. I've met his family. I've been to his home. You guys are so overreacting."

"If we are, it's about not wanting you to get hurt," Becca said. "That's all."

"I'd say any hurting going on will happen in the pit with everyone moshing." Milla forced a laugh. "I'll be perfectly safe with Rennie."

"If you say so," Risa finally said, giving her a quick hug. The others followed suit. Milla loved her friends but wished they'd leave her alone about this. Especially about this. The last thing she wanted was for them to accuse her of protesting too much.

She waved as they scurried off, and turned to walk back to where Rennie lay sprawled on his side, taking up half of the blanket she'd spread on the ground earlier.

Seeing his legs so long and thick in his faded jeans, his white T-shirt teasing her with the way it hinted at the amazing muscles in both his arms and his chest…

A shiver ran down her spine as she waited for him to spot her, wondering what he'd do when he did, how he'd react. She didn't have long to wait.

He pushed back a sweep of dark hair from his forehead before reaching for his beer. He drank, meeting her gaze over the rim of the plastic cup, lowering it slowly as he watched her approach.

His eyes never left her, his body never moved. He stared as if he'd never seen her before. As if she was exactly what he wanted, what he dreamed of, and she would vanish if he dared to look away.

God, this was insane. She shouldn't want to be with him the way that she did. This longing was what she should've felt for Derek. She didn't understand any of what was going on. All she knew was that this was a heady feeling, meaning this much to Rennie.

She dropped her gaze, uncertain what to say to him, saved from having to say anything by the roar of the crowd because just as she reached the blanket, Incubus took the stage. Along with the rest of the whistling, cheering, screaming fans, Rennie stood.

The crowd stayed on its feet dancing from the beginning of "Shaft" to the end, then settled down for the show. Milla did the same, swaying side to side, pungently sweet smoke drifting to her on the breeze.

"You didn't have to stay with me," Rennie leaned in to whisper. His breath was warm and smelled of beer, his hair smelled of shampoo, his shirt of sunshine.

She shivered, shook her head. "I wasn't in the mood to be crushed in the pit."

He laughed, the sound seeming to press against her neck like the edge of a knife. "And here I thought you stayed so I wouldn't be alone."

He frightened her. He excited her. The things he said. The looks he gave her. His tone of voice totally contradicting what she'd seen in his eyes.

Two could play at this game, she mused, leaning toward him to say, "For some reason, I don't think of you as needing a sitter," before dropping back to the blanket.

He followed her down. "Rumor has it I could use someone to keep me in line."

The same rumors her girlfriends had dangled in front of her earlier. She lifted a brow, glanced over. "Good luck with that."

"I was thinking of offering you the job." He reached

up, toyed with the ends of her hair. "Derek doesn't seem to need you to keep an eye on him."

The truth in Rennie's words stung, and she started to pull away, not caring that just minutes ago being with him was the only thing on her mind. Why did he have to be so cruel…so honest?

He stopped her, moving in behind her, pressing his body to hers where they sat in the dark on her blanket. It was hard to think when he was so large and so close, when he warmed her skin where she'd grown cold.

"Derek's a big boy," she finally said. "He doesn't need a keeper."

"Are you sure about that?" Rennie dropped his chin to her shoulder.

She didn't want to talk about Derek; why was he talking about Derek? She wanted to pretend for just tonight that she was free. "I'm not going to start doubting Derek just because of what we've done."

Rennie laughed, the sound wicked and deep. "I'm pretty damn sure what we do isn't the same as what you do with him. You ever show him how much fun you can have with your car's gearshift knob?"

"Oh, don't even go there." And yet again she was protesting too much. "It was your fault I got stuck between the seats."

"Maybe. But you liked it." He nipped at her earlobe. "You even begged."

"I did not beg." Not out loud, anyway, she admitted to herself, reaching up to push him away.

"Liar," he said, reading her mind.

He wasn't playing games at all. He was forcing her to look at herself more closely than was comfortable, and suddenly all she wanted to do was go home. "I think this was a mistake. Staying here. I should go find Derek."

"No. Stay with me," Rennie said, the tone of his voice demanding yet…something else, something more. She heard panic, fear, a strange distress. As if the thought of her leaving hurt him.

She'd tried to leave him before. She hated sneaking around. Hated giving in to this obsession that she didn't understand. The guilt that ate at her was a living, breathing thing, but it didn't seem to matter. She always came back. He fed her soul. He made her ache with being alive. Her time with him mattered to her more than anything in her life had ever mattered before.

So instead of pushing him away, she found herself saying, "Okay."

She stayed, and she did so without putting any distance between them. When she moved to the music, he moved, too, his chest pressed to her back, the hand bearing his weight dangerously close to her hip.

God, who was she kidding? He was dangerously close all over. His body heat, his scent, his bulk that she could feel each time he swayed and leaned near.

She wrapped her arms over her chest and hugged herself tightly, wanting things she didn't understand, things she was certain she shouldn't be wanting at all—especially from Rennie.

Not when she knew next to nothing about him. Or

so little about herself. Not when the voice inside her head was insisting that her feelings were wrong. She couldn't help any of it, not the physical sensations tightening her body, or those that were tied to her heart.

Derek had so many friends she often felt like an afterthought, a convenience. She came from money, just as he did. She had the family name that complimented his own. They were the perfect Ken and Barbie of their social set.

What Rennie made her feel was rich and deep and frightening in its importance. He made her feel as if she mattered. She ached with wanting to understand why. He was so different from Derek, from any guy she'd ever thought about dating, from all the guys she hung out with.

He came from a place she knew little about, a place where money *was* an object, where getting by required more than the right family name. He was the only one of Derek's friends who held down a job while going to school. He was the only one who had to.

It was as if having been born into two different worlds, they had found each other here in a third while finding themselves, as well.

The crowd getting to their feet distracted her from further musings. The night had grown cold and dark, and when she shivered, Rennie grabbed the wrap from the ground, tossed it around his shoulders, and bundled her up in the cocoon of the blanket and his body.

He held the edges together in front of her, leaving her hands free to roam. She started with his arms, stroking her fingers over his wrists and up to his elbows, marveling at how soft she found his skin when he appeared to be so hard.

She leaned her head back into the crook of his shoulder and slipped her hands beneath his T-shirt sleeves, pushing her thumbs into the taut bulge of his biceps. He groaned, and so she pushed harder, feeling her way along his tendons and bones.

"Don't do that, Milla." He whispered the words into her ear. "Not if you don't want to go there."

She wasn't sure what she wanted, what she was doing except for what felt right. She lifted one hand up to his neck, threaded her fingers into his hair, toyed with his ear and pulled his head closer.

"Shh," she said. "Don't talk. Just listen to the band."

It was as if she and Rennie were all alone, the music playing for no one else as the blanket enveloped them and the darkness swallowed them up. She couldn't remember a night in her past so perfect.

She wanted to hold her breath, to never move again, to let the music take her away. She wanted to stand here and pretend that nothing mattered beyond these stolen moments with Rennie.

He shifted his weight, holding the bunched edges of the blanket in place with one hand, freeing his other and moving it to her stomach, spreading his fingers wide and pushing her back into the cradle he'd made of his body.

His palm caught her T-shirt hem. His fingertips settled on the strip of skin bared beneath. A shiver tickled the base of her skull, sliding down her spine until it settled in the small of her back. She wiggled against him, felt the swell behind his zipper as his cock came to life.

Her own desire rose just as swiftly, swiftly enough to steal away her breath. She inhaled shakily and covered his hand where he stroked her belly, threading their fingers together and urging him down until the heat of his palm grazed the skin between her legs.

She moaned quietly, and he let loose a sound that she felt more than heard, a low gritty growl that her body absorbed, that made her ache and grow wet.

She wore little beneath her short denim skirt, just a tiny scrap of white cotton. She released his hand and wriggled out of her panties, shoving them in Rennie's front pocket since she had no pocket of her own.

Thinking about what she was doing wasn't even on her radar. This was all about what Rennie made her feel, and her very desperate need for him to make her come. He whispered all sorts of things under his breath, cursing her, cursing himself, angrily damning the time and the place, sharing her lack of control.

"Hold the blanket," he ordered, wedging his knee between hers and nudging her legs apart.

She gripped the edges tightly together, and when Rennie pulled up her skirt, her knees began to tremble. His hands were hot against the backs of her thighs, and then against her bottom.

He slipped the length of one index finger between her legs, sliding it between her folds. His other hand he settled low on her belly, his fingers tangling in her damp curls as he searched out the hard bud of her clit.

He fingered her from behind, played her from the front, brought her to the edge of orgasm over and over again. Each time he backed off she wanted to scream, until he finally pulled his fingers from inside her and pushed her T-shirt and sweater up and out of the way.

Still cupping her sex with one hand, he toyed with her breasts with the other, tugging at her nipples until she felt a sharp pull and clenched her thighs in response. She couldn't believe this was happening. That he was making her hurt so good, that she was so desperate to have him.

"I want you in my mouth," he said, kneading her breasts, pinching her nipples, sliding the fingers of his other hand deep inside her again. "I want to taste all of you. To lick you and suck you. To taste you and drink you up."

She couldn't wait any longer. She came in his hand, riding the stroking rhythm he set. She shuddered, lost her balance, felt like she was going to die. He held her tight, didn't let her fall, refused to let her go.

He stayed with her all the while and never rushed her, making sure she was finished, not asking her for a thing. His thoughtfulness nearly brought her to tears, and she said, "I need to feel you inside, Rennie. Please. Now."

She shouldn't have been able to hear anything above the band or the crowd singing along. She shouldn't have been able to hear the sharp breath he sucked back, or the rasp of his zipper coming undone, but she did.

She heard it all and was ready when he dipped his

knees behind her. She arched her back and spread her legs, giving him access, holding the blanket close. He was so hot, his skin so tight where he rubbed the head of his cock against the crease between her ass and the top of her thigh.

He filled her slowly, stretching her open, easing inside with almost no outward motion at all. They looked no different from the rest of the crowd. They were just another couple, huddled close beneath a blanket for warmth, moving to the music's sexy beat.

Rennie pulled out slowly, pushed back in, wrapping an arm around her waist to hold her where he wanted her. She closed her eyes, disappeared inside herself, felt nothing but the way he stirred her and brought her body to life.

He slipped his hand at her waist lower, pulling back her folds with his first two fingers and spreading her open around his shaft. She bit back a moan and shuddered, her belly tightening, her sex tightening, too.

"Hold on," he said, seconds later, driving into her so hard he nearly took her off her feet. She felt him pulse and heat, and she came again in response, contracting around him as she burst and saw stars.

It seemed to take forever for her to return to solid ground. And it was only later that she wondered how something so very wrong could seem more right than anything she'd known in her life.

"WHAT DO YOU THINK would have happened if we hadn't gotten so carried away at that Incubus concert?"

"What kind of question is that?" Rennie responded, gazing at Milla from over the rim of his wineglass. He didn't want to say anything to darken the mood any further now that they'd made it out of his car and into the club she'd been assigned to review.

It was a fairly swanky place called Test Flight. A half-moon bar hugged a circular dance floor that was lit by colored strobes from above. Clusters of both high and low tables sat off to one side.

The art on the walls, abstract and expressionist, was reminiscent of Jackson Pollack—a fact Rennie knew because an ex-girlfriend had run Ed Harris's film about the artist's life constantly.

Nothing about any of that or about any of the beautiful people milling around set this place apart from others with a similar atmosphere. He was pretty sure what did—and what Milla's Web site was looking to profile—were the second-floor balcony seats.

They sat in one of the booths even now. The dividing walls between each were high, the table long and narrow, allowing for a single bench seat on only one side. Both ends were open—one looking out over the dance floor, the other giving the servers access—though both came with privacy drapes.

Milla reached over, pulled theirs wider before she gave him a reply. "The same kind of question as any other. The kind that deserves an answer."

Obviously she wasn't going to let him off the hook. "I was hoping it was rhetorical."

She shifted on the seat they shared to face him and

lifted a brow. "You were hoping to have fun without having to talk."

That much he couldn't deny. Still… "If you mean the fun we had in your kitchen, I never expected that to happen at all."

"Honestly? Neither did I," she said, glancing down at her drink. "Though I can't say I'm totally surprised that it did."

Interesting. Especially since she'd been the one to whisper into his ear. "You didn't want it to happen?"

She looked back up. "If I hadn't wanted it to happen, it wouldn't have. But sex wasn't the reason I came to see you yesterday."

"Are you ever going to tell me what was?" He still wasn't convinced about the business card thing.

"I did." She raised her glass and grinned. "That's why we're here."

Had he actually forgotten what an expert tease she was? Or how he felt like a sap for letting her get to him? "I don't mean you needing a date. I don't believe for a minute you had to look me up to have someone to go out with."

She laughed. "The dating-for-a-living life is not all fun and games. Anyway, you still haven't answered me."

A tenacious tease at that. He took a long swallow of his wine. "The concert was nothing, Milla. Things were going to get out of control sooner or later. You knew it as well as I did."

"Do you ever regret what we did?" she asked, her thumb toying with the bowl of her glass.

He shook his head. "I never do anything that I'll later regret."

"But how can you know at the time?" She looked up sharply, her voice taking on a strangely desperate tone. "Things change. We change. Our priorities. Our perceptions of others."

He wondered what her regrets were…and if they included him. "At the core? I don't believe we change at all."

She smiled softly, dipped the tip of her finger into her drink. "Does that mean you'll spend your life yearning to see the world and seek your fortune?"

He really did hate having words from all those years ago coming back to bite him in the butt. If he continued to deceive her about who he was, things were going to get sticky. But since he had no idea if this was going to turn into more than a temporarily rekindled sexual relationship, he kept his mouth shut.

At least until he found a viable change of subject. "How much of it have you seen? Or have you stuck close to home all this time?"

Her smile faded, and her knuckles turned white when she wrapped her fingers around her drink. "I started work right after graduation, and eventually ended up at MatchMeUp. I've never had time for a real vacation."

"In six years?"

She shrugged. "I know. You don't have to tell me how pathetic that sounds."

Pathetic wasn't the word he'd have chosen, but it did

fit with his assessment that something in Milla's world wasn't quite right. "If you could go anywhere, where would it be?"

She shook her head. "I don't even have time to think about a vacation. Not with things at work so shaky right now."

He'd get back to the work thing later. "Make time. For me. Anywhere in the world, where would you go?"

She blew out a breath, shook back her hair. "God, you'll think I'm so lame."

"How so?" he asked, frowning.

"Because honestly? I'd like to stay right here. At home."

"Home? As in San Francisco?"

"Oh, no." The light returned to her eyes as she took a quick sip of her drink and set her glass on the table. "The whole United States. Like live in an RV for a year and just drive."

It would be so easy for him to make that happen. What wasn't quite as easy was explaining to himself why his thoughts had even gone there. Except for the obvious scenario involving him, wrapping, and her little finger.

And then he remembered something. "What happened to the money you were coming into after graduation? You blow it all on wine, men and song?"

"No. Just my apartment. I got tired of renting."

She wasn't telling him everything, but he didn't think this was the time to pry. "Judging by the neighborhood and what I saw of your place, you won't have any problem coming up with RV money if you decide to sell."

She huffed. "If our office closes and I lose my job, I might have to sell to keep myself from living out of a cardboard box in the Tenderloin."

He frowned, studying the shadows beneath her eyes. "Is there a chance of that happening? Not you ending up on the streets, but the office closing?"

"Honestly? I don't think so, but so much of our revenue comes from advertising, and it seems we're suddenly not edgy enough. Our ad revenues are down." She drained her drink.

He signaled for their server. "And reviewing clubs like this one fill that bill?"

"According to our orders from headquarters…yes," she said, following the direction of his gaze across the open space above the dance floor, and into the booths on the other side of the club's second floor where not everyone cared to make use of the booth's curtains.

Who needed adult films when there were live adults putting on a show? No one was naked. It was all discreet. But it was obvious, for example, that the guy in the booth directly across from theirs—the one with the tablecloth draped over his lap and the female partner who'd just slipped underneath—would be going home a happy man.

Rennie's mind went to Milla where she'd leaned into the curve of his chest. He could smell her scent, feel her body's heat, and he remembered how it felt to have her mouth on him. How it felt to be buried inside of her.

He cleared his throat and put a bit of distance between them, dropping his head against the booth's padded top. Milla turned, crossed her legs, and angled her body toward his as she asked, "Are you okay?"

No, he wanted to say. *I need you to climb out of your clothes and into my lap.* But he didn't. What he said instead was, "I'm guessing in the case of your advertisers that edgy means sexy."

She gave a hedging nod, tucked strands of hair behind her ear. "Sex sells movies, books, even cars and cleaning products. Using it to sell a dating service makes good business sense."

His frustration grew worse by the minute and, prick that he was, he took it out on the source. "Don't you already do that by default? When you hook people up? Isn't that using sex as a selling point?"

She waited until their server had exchanged empty glasses for full before responding. "Some clients use our services for finding companions with similar interests."

He snorted. "Right. And that interest would be sex."

"Not always," she insisted. "Some like the proverbial long walks on the beach—"

"Ending in sex—"

"Some like quiet evenings spent listening to guitarists in coffee houses—"

"Followed by sex—"

"Some like a nice dinner, a movie, intelligent conversation—"

"Topped off by wild and crazy monkey sex."

She paused, tilted her head to the side and studied

his expression, which no doubt appeared as pissy as he felt. "Is that all you think about?"

He knocked back the rest of his drink. "I'm not the one matchmaking for a living."

"I don't matchmake. I do club and restaurant reviews."

He was angry. He shouldn't be. But even going into tonight with his eyes wide open, he hated feeling used. Hated letting her do it to him again. "Why haven't you found a match for yourself?"

"What?" Her face paled.

"You have access to tens of thousands of eligible men. Yet you come to me for a date. Why aren't you in a relationship, Milla? It was so important to you in college to stay with Derek even though the two of you didn't work the way the two of us did."

She couldn't even look him in the eyes. "That was a long time ago, Rennie. Being with Derek then was...right."

"And being with me was wrong."

"It *was* wrong," she said, her voice cracking. "The way we did it. Everything about it was wrong."

"Except the sex."

"Especially the sex. You know that."

"No, Milla. Everything about it was right." He dug into his wallet to settle their bill. "It was right. And telling yourself anything else is a lie."

7

"HEY, CHICA, wait up."

At the sound of Amy Child's voice, Milla stopped and turned in time to see her coworker scurry off the elevator and down the hall.

As usual, Amy had waited until the last possible minute to heft her eight-month pregnant bulk out of her chair, and was now scrambling to get to a working bathroom before it was too late.

Milla chuckled, shaking her head. "Hurry up, Momma Childs. It's booty call time, and you'll be lucky to get a stall."

Amy waved a hand. "Then go. Hurry. Run interference for me."

By the time Milla reached the door and pulled it open, Amy was on her heels barreling through. Milla followed, turning toward the lounge where several of the sisters had gathered for Monday's lottery.

A couple of the women laughed as Amy zipped by, Jo Ann from the travel agency saying, "Damn, but I am feeling her pain. My bladder has not been the same since the birth of number two."

Milla settled into one of the chairs and joined in as the volume of the good-natured chatter rose. Finally, Cherie Glass, one of the interns from Dillard Marketing who had a family wedding to attend and wanted an escort, drew the first card from the boot.

Her co-worker, Danica Lanston, immediately pounced. "Read the back. I love seeing what my sisters have said about the men they've donated to the cause."

"Donated?" Teena, one of the financial consultants from the fifteenth floor, gave a derisive snort from the corner of the sofa where she lounged like a queen. "I'm not sure if discarded wouldn't be a better description. I have come up with nothing but losers digging in that thing."

Milla figured she was thinking what the rest of the group was thinking—that Teena's lack of success in dating had little to do with the cards in the boot and a lot to do with her attitude.

"I've had a dud or two," Milla decided to offer as she remembered last week's life-of-the-cruise-ship-party guy. And then she thought of Rennie. "But I've also made a decent hook-up."

"Recently?" asked Pamela Hoff, Teena's statuesque coworker, her platinum ringlets as perfectly coiffed as her figure was curvy.

Milla nodded, breaking into a giveaway grin that had the women whooping and hollering and speculating on her orgasms and the size of the man involved.

"From that look on your face I'm guessing you won't be dipping into the kitty today," Julia Nguyen said.

"No, she won't." At the sound of Natalie's voice, Milla glanced up as her friend joined the group. "My girl has too much work to do and no time for men."

"Wait," Danica said. "Cherie still hasn't read the note on the back of her card. Just because I have a date this weekend with my DVD player and Russell Crowe doesn't mean I don't need a vicarious thrill."

"Okay, okay," Cherie said nervously, her spiky hair the color of a grape Popsicle. "Here goes. 'If all you want is a good time with a big spender, go for it. But know the man is allergic to rings.'"

"O-oh."

"Ow."

"That's brutal."

"Hey, it's fine by me," Cherie insisted, waving the card like a fan. "I only need one date for the wedding. Not fifty years. Besides, spending big usually means he's compensating for a lack somewhere else."

"Ain't that the truth," Teena said, clicking her tongue. "Like size doesn't matter. The motion of the ocean don't mean a thing if you can't find the friggin' boat."

After that, everyone began to talk at once, adding their two cents to the collective opinion that when it came to permanence, financial stability mattered even more than a man's grasp of the female anatomy, or the size of what he used to sail the high seas.

Looking around at the women in the room, most who she knew only casually, Milla thought back to the words that had been jotted on Rennie's card and was struck with a sharp twinge of jealousy.

Great eyes? Check. Incredible smile? Check. Body to make a girl melt inside? Check, check, check. Potential for high yield capital gains? No, but he's hell on wheels in bed. And really, isn't that all that matters?

Who here had been with him to know what it was like to share his bed? Who had judged him by his financial portfolio and decided he wasn't good enough except as a sexual partner?

No one here except Amy and Natalie knew who she'd gone out with, and neither one of her coworkers knew the full truth of her and Rennie's past.

But she was caught off guard by the hurt that sliced through her at the thought of Rennie facing rejection by one of these women because he was blue-collar instead of blue blood.

The urge to jump to his defense struck her hard. Did the fact that he worked with his hands instead of on Wall Street truly matter?

She couldn't imagine judging a man by his bank account instead of taking into consideration the whole of who he was—a thought that took her back to school and the night that had ended what she'd had with Rennie.

She would never forget how Derek and his friends had laughed in Rennie's face for thinking a rich girl like Milla would have anything to do with a broke loser, grease monkey like him.

Even worse was being unable to forget that she'd let them—and how she'd never said a word.

NOON ON MONDAY FOUND Rennie standing just inside
the garage bay watching Hector welding in the yard.
Sparks popped, reflecting off the welding hood protect-
ing the other man's eyes.

Behind Rennie in the garage, Jin called orders to his
two-man crew. Air compressors blasted. The rev and
roar of power tools cycled up and down. Metal giving
way creaked and moaned.

Rennie heard it all the same way he heard the phone
ringing. It registered as background noise and nothing
more. These were the sounds he heard every day, had
been hearing all of his life.

He was comfortable here, in his element, surrounded by all the things with which he was so familiar.
This was the place he called home.

The one downside to his celebrity was the publicity,
the appearances he had to make, the autograph hounds.
He knew it came with the territory, but it was his least
favorite part of the job.

At heart, he was just a guy lucky enough to do what
he loved to do for a living. The fact that the cars he
restored were anything but average, and he did it all
for a television audience—not to mention for a bundle
of cash—was a bonus. One he had mixed feelings
about, taking the good with the annoyance of the papa-
razzi.

He wondered what Milla would think if she knew
who he really was, what he did, how much he was
worth these days. Would it make a difference in how
she saw him now? In what she wanted from him? Or

would he still be a convenient date and a cheap and easy lay?

He propped his hand overhead on the rolling door's frame and bit off a self-directed curse. He couldn't believe he cared what Milla thought. Not after all this time. They'd had no contact since college. He'd never thought he'd see her again.

And the first time he gets her alone, what does he do? Yeah, sure, she was right there with him. She was, in fact, the one who'd invited him to take a ride.

But son of a barking dog if he wasn't out of his mind to climb behind the wheel when she was an accident waiting to happen.

No woman had ever worked her way under his skin the way Milla had. He'd used his trip around the world after graduation to get her out of his head. Yet the minute he saw her again—

A loud crash behind him had him swinging around in time to see Jin deliver a swift kick to the light he'd obviously backed into and knocked to the ground.

Shooting for the upcoming season of Hell on Wheels was being done in stages as Rennie and his team worked through transforming the individual machines.

Practically, it made more sense to finish one project before moving on to the next. Realistically, he ran into problems that took time to solve, making an assembly-line scenario impossible.

While he was dealing with one issue, Jin would follow up on another, and Hector would work out the fine print on a third. Obviously things with Jin's crew weren't going too well today.

Rennie welcomed the change of subject from brooding over Milla to work, but had only made it halfway across the garage when Hector's, "Yo, Ren," stopped him.

"What's up?" he called, heading back the way he'd come.

His welding hood under his arm, Hector gestured over his shoulder. "The weld's a good one, but I'm running a pressure test anyway. Dropping the submersible and having it leak ain't gonna win you many fans."

Rennie snorted. "Are you kidding? They love it when we screw up as much as when we get it right."

Hector ran a red shop rag over his neck and head to soak up the sweat. "Maybe. Guess I'm still stuck back in the days when a paycheck meant a guy didn't stop until a job was done right."

"In our business, I figure all we can do is try," Rennie said with a laugh.

Hector jerked upright when another loud bang echoed through the bay. "It don't look like Jin's trying is going so well."

Rennie followed the direction of Hector's gaze. "Just wait till the crew starts up filming again."

Hector stared toward the front of the garage. "You think his wife's going to keep giving him hell about the groupies until he quits the show?"

"I don't think he'll quit. But I don't think she will,

either," Rennie said, his thoughts drifting to Milla and their years of indiscretion, her infidelity, his betrayal of a friend, hers, too.

"Women." Hector shoved his rag in his shirt pocket. "I'm beginning to wonder if they're worth it."

Rennie cast a glance at the other man. In all the years Hector had been working at Bergen Motors, Rennie had never seen him serious with anyone. "You having love troubles?"

"It ain't love, man, and I doubt it ever will be since I'm stuck on figuring out what they want."

"Well, you can start with treating them nice." *Not attacking them on their kitchen table then making cruel accusations because frustration's eating you alive.*

Hector rolled his eyes. "Is that the best you can do?"

"Just stating the obvious." *Since I obviously need the reminder,* Rennie mused, his gut tightening with the apology he owed Milla.

"Yeah, well, I didn't think it was going to be this hard."

Rennie was more than willing to be distracted by Hector's problems instead of his own. "So who's got your goat?"

Hector tossed his welding hood onto the worktable. "Like I'm gonna share the goings-on of my social life with you."

"You gonna bring her to Thanksgiving dinner at my folks'?"

"Who, Ang—?" Hector reddened and hung his head. "Crap."

"You and Angie? As in Angela Soon? The terror of the time cards? The feared one of the filing system? The ogre of organization?"

Hector rubbed at his forehead as if trying to get rid of a pain. "That would be her."

Rennie chuckled. "And right beneath my nose, too."

"It hasn't been going on long. And it's not like it's really going on at all. We went to dinner on Friday. That's it."

"Angie's not the easiest girl to get a handle on."

"Her mother made me dessert. Without never even meeting me. I don't know if she was thanking me for getting her daughter out of the house or what."

Rennie laughed. "Man, I wouldn't want to walk three feet in your shoes."

"What, like you're some Casanova or something? I don't see you dating none of the chicks who just happen by when the show's filming."

"I don't know any of those chicks."

"And you don't get to know them, either." Hector's dark gaze narrowed. "Unless this is about that chick who came by to see you last week."

Was nothing that went on in his life sacred? Rennie turned his attention back to Jin. "I'm not having this conversation."

"Angie was right."

Rennie listened to another round of Jin's yelling. "You and Angie spend your time together talking about me?"

"What else do we got to talk about? You're the only thing we've got in common."

"Great. Now I'm going to be blamed for ruining your relationship."

"We don't got no relationship, man. We just went out the once." Hector paused. "Hey. Don't you got a policy against employees dating?"

"You want me to start one?" Rennie asked, thinking it was too little too late.

"I'll let you know," Hector said as the office phone resumed ringing. "I'll get that."

Rennie nodded. "Thanks. I need to put Jin in time-out and see what's going on."

"Fifty bucks, he's got his woman on his mind," Hector said, jogging toward the office.

Didn't they all, Rennie mused, ready to smack himself around. Getting his head off of Milla and back in the game had to happen soon, else he'd find himself in a time-out of his own.

The thing was, if what he and Milla had shared in the past had been intended to be permanent—or be more than sex—they wouldn't have so easily lost their way. They wouldn't have drifted apart.

And it sure as hell didn't take a genius IQ to know that what they had now, or what they'd done Friday night, was no deeper or more meaningful than what had gone before.

Sex and lies might draw in big box-office numbers, but it never worked in real life. At least not in the sort of life Rennie wanted to live. He'd been there in college. He'd done that with her then.

Even worse, he was doing it again now, not telling

her the truth about who he was, yet banging her brains out the first time he got her alone.

So why if he knew all of that to be true was he so desperate to see her again? That might be the question of the day, but he didn't like the implications of the answer.

He refused to admit that he'd been in love with her all of these years. Instead, he did what he did best and got back to work.

BY THE TIME Hector reached the office, the phone had stopped ringing. He didn't bother to check the voice mail; whoever it was could call back.

While he waited, he stood in front of the floor fan trying to cool off, sweating like a pig, and fighting the part of the heat that came straight from his chat with Rennie.

He wanted to kick himself for letting on that he'd gone out with Angie. They hadn't talked about staying quiet. And really, there wasn't much to say, or much of a secret to keep. It had only been one date.

Still, he hadn't yet worked out what he was thinking about the whole thing, and he wanted to do that before he did anything else. Otherwise, he was going to ask her out again before deciding if it was a smart thing to do.

They'd had a good time. At least he had, and he thought she'd enjoyed herself, too. The food at the place she'd picked out had been great. It was the kind of food he didn't eat very often seeing as how he didn't cook. Half the time when he got home at night he was too tired to make more than a sandwich.

It had been fun to watch Angie eat. She'd talked the whole time, and she'd had more than a few of the other people around them watching her, too. Not because she was loud or had bad manners or anything, but because she was…real. He couldn't think of any other way to describe it.

She ate like she was hungry. She talked like she had something to say, using her hands, her eyes flashing. And when she laughed, anyone who heard her knew she meant business.

Hector had been hard half the night, and he was pretty damn certain he wasn't the only one, judging by the strain on some of the male faces around them—and by the scowls a few of the women wore.

When they'd got back to her house after eating and he'd walked her to her front door, that had been it. The end of the night. She'd told him she'd had a wonderful time, that she'd see him Monday, and had gone inside.

He hadn't tried to kiss her or anything. He might have if she'd hesitated before opening the door. She hadn't, so he'd turned and gone home.

And to keep from wondering how things would go down when he saw her again on Monday, he'd spent the rest of the weekend working on the submersible at the garage.

He needed sleep. He needed a vacation. A lot of days off to do nothing but chill. Maybe take a long overdue trip to see his family. But right now more than anything, he needed a cold shower. He was so freaking hot.

"Is there a reason you people down here can't answer the phone? It's not like I have nothing to do but run back and forth from the showroom to deliver your messages."

Hector didn't even open his eyes. He just stood there in front of the fan and grinned. "Hey, Ang. How goes your Monday?"

She didn't answer. She just stepped between him and his fan. He didn't even have to look up to see. He knew because he lost most of the breeze. And because what breeze he could feel smelled just like Angie, all flowery and sweet.

"I am overworked and underpaid. That's how my Monday is going."

"You could've left a voice mail." He stepped around her to check the phone. "I don't see no red light blinking."

And that was when he finally took her in. All of her. The blue dress she wore with ruffles along the neckline. The matching four-inch stilettos. The flower tucked behind her ear and into the coil of her black hair.

His grin became a smile that he felt with his body even more than he felt with his face. "You got any more complaints? I'll be happy to talk to the boss."

"The Captain is trying to reach Rennie. He's got another frame he thinks will work, but wants a commitment before he sets it aside."

"Ren ain't gonna commit to nothing until he sees it or sends Jin over to take a look." But then Angie knew all of that, and could have said as much to the Captain herself. There wasn't a reason Hector could think of for her to deliver the message herself.

Unless… "Was there something else, Angie? Something you needed to come all the way down here to say? You know, instead of leaving a message?"

She pressed her bare lips together, crossed her arms over the ruffles hiding her breasts. "Yeah. Do you want anything for lunch? I was going out for a burger, and thought I'd bring you one if you haven't eaten yet. If you're hungry."

"I am," he said, and left it at that because he felt a lot of things stirring he wasn't ready to tell her he felt. "Do you want me to check with the other guys?"

"No." She shook her head. "I don't have that many hands. Or that much money."

He liked that she was making excuses. If she called in a big enough order, she could get the food delivered. She knew that having done it a bunch of times before.

He dug for his wallet. "Here, let me—"

"I got it," she said, cutting him off. "You paid for the lasagna. This is my treat."

He frowned. "I thought the apple crisp was your treat."

"That was my mamma's."

"Okay, but that means you have to let me buy dinner this weekend."

"If we keep going back and forth, we'll never be even," she said, her voice sharp and tight.

Hmm. He didn't get where she was coming from. "Why do we have to be even?"

"Because I don't like being in debt, or owing anything to anyone."

He came out from behind the desk then and walked toward her, knowing he smelled like oil and grease and sweat, yet stopping only when he was so close that she had to look up. "Me buying you dinner doesn't put you in my debt, Angie. That's a really strange way of looking at friendship."

He watched her throat work when she swallowed. "I wasn't sure if that's what you were thinking. Or if you were wanting…"

"Wanting to be more? I'd say it's too soon for either of us to know that, wouldn't you?"

She nodded her head briskly. "I would. But I've known other people—"

"Other guys, you mean?"

She nodded again. "I've known other guys who thought if they bought me dinner, then they'd bought me for the night."

Things were finally making sense. "Is that why you hurried inside after I walked you home on Friday? You thought I was going to expect something from you?"

Her chin came up higher. "I only know you from work, Hector. People aren't always the same in other situations as when you're working with them."

She was only being honest. He had no reason to feel hurt. "Did you think I was different? Was that me any different from this me?"

She tilted her head one way then the other before she scrunched up her nose. "The other you smelled better."

He laughed. "The other me hadn't been underneath a welding hood all day, working up a hell of an appetite."

Her eyes widened and got all bright and flashy. "I forgot about the food. I'll go get it now."

"Not yet," he said, reaching a second time for his wallet. He handed her thirty bucks and gave her his order. "Get whatever you want, and bring me the change."

"No. I'm paying."

"No. You're not."

"You're awfully bossy for someone who's not the boss."

"Who I am is the guy who is going to prove to you that we don't all expect something in return for everything we do. Some of us just like to be nice."

She stared at the money she held for several seconds, then folded it up and tucked it into her bra as if it were the most normal thing in the world to do. She tickled him, this Angela Soon, so comfortable with herself, yet so prickly.

"I'll be back as soon as I can," she said, and took a step toward the door.

"Sounds good to me," he answered, watching her go.

She hesitated; he wasn't sure why, and he frowned, staying where he was and staying silent, waiting while she made up her mind. When she finally did, she walked back to where he stood, took hold of his wrist and rose up on tiptoe, kissing him full on the lips.

"Thank you, Hector."

"For what?" he asked, too stunned to say more.

"For being one of the nice guys." With that, she spun around and sashayed out of the office, leaving him unable to breathe, and barely able to stand.

And so he sat. Hard. Right on the edge of the desk, knocking the fan to the floor.

8

MIDWAY THROUGH the week, Milla found herself unable to concentrate on anything work related. It was as if she'd developed a sudden case of aphasia. No matter the time she spent focused on writing her review, her brain refused to cooperate. The clever turns of phrase she was known for just wouldn't come.

This job was slowly becoming as boring as the first one she'd had out of college where she'd been hired to manage the office of a high-profile San Francisco real-estate broker and had spent more time at the switchboard instead. She'd lasted two years, learning of the opening at MatchMeUpOnline.com when buying ad space for the broker in their Web site's classifieds.

The new job at MatchMeUp involved coordinating all their marketing plans as well as writing copy. Her flair with words had soon gotten her noticed. She'd been doing the club and restaurant reviews for the past two years now—though she doubted she'd be doing them much longer considering she'd forgotten how to write.

Test Flight had opened in several cities around the

country two weeks before, and was being billed by the owners as the perfect spot to give a first date a spin. She supposed it worked in theory. The club's main floor allowed couples to rev up their engines, drinking and dancing and finding their groove, while the upstairs booths provided intimacy for those ready to experience takeoff.

There was only one problem with translating the experience for visitors to the site. She couldn't find the right words to describe it. Oh, sure. She'd detailed the lighting, the sound system, the attentiveness of the servers and the drinks. But how was she supposed to recommend the club for its first date appeal when the night had been a reunion not a trial run?

And her state of mind had only gotten worse since Monday morning's booty call. She was ridiculously obsessed with wanting to know which of the sisters had dropped Rennie's card into the vase, but she didn't want to ask and have to explain her interest.

It was bad enough to admit to herself that she was jealous, but there it was. She couldn't stand the fact that one of the women who worked in her building knew him as intimately as she did—even while she couldn't believe the other woman knew him at all.

Still, the thought that someone with whom she was acquainted had slept with him nearly killed her, and reinforced the obvious. She was going totally insane. She had no rights as far as he was concerned, no claim on any part of his life.

Even in college she and Rennie had never committed to an emotional involvement. They hadn't even bothered to keep in touch since graduation—she hadn't kept in touch with any of her friends—and their sexual affair was a thing of the past. Or it had been. Until Friday.

And now that Rennie had agreed to join her on this second review date, she couldn't stop thinking about the Friday night to come.

In fact, Wednesday evening she ended up making a complete mess of her bedroom, pulling items from her closet that she hadn't worn in years, seeing what still fit, what emphasized her meager proportions, what looked like crap—and wondering when she'd so fully embraced all things black.

Her wardrobe could have outfitted the patrons in two goth clubs and an emo bar thrown in for good measure. Ugh, what in the world was wrong with her? Black was so not her color. How could she have gone over to the dark side without even noticing?

What did that say about her life? And was whatever it said what Rennie meant about her having been broken?

Before she could agonize further, her cell phone rang, keeping her from suffering more self-analysis. Kept her, too, from loading everything she owned into garbage bags and heading for the dump.

She answered without bothering to look at the incoming number. "Hello?"

"Are we still on for Friday night?"

At the sound of Rennie's gruffly voiced question,

she closed her eyes and sank to the edge of the bed. "Unless you're bailing on me. Which I really need to know. So I can find a replacement."

"Replace me? Seriously? You haven't managed it yet, have you?"

Damn him for being who he was, for being so right, so confident. She just wished they'd had some sort of normal beginning. That everything about their time together hadn't been a lie. "I guess that's a no, then? You're not canceling?"

He gave a halfhearted laugh. "And miss out on another chance to dissect the past?"

His sarcasm wasn't lost on her. "You're the one who brought up the past, remember? I was happy to keep strictly to the present."

"Right. All business. Nothing personal."

"I was up front about that going in," she reminded him, plopping back onto the bed.

He didn't say anything for several seconds, and she imagined him frowning as he worked out whatever it was he was thinking. "Were you looking to buy a car?"

She switched the phone to her other ear, pushed her hair out of the way. "No, why?"

"I'm still trying to figure out how you ran across my card."

"I found it at work," she said, wondering how much she should reveal about the sisters and the booty call Mondays. "We have a collection of business cards in a vase in one of the ladies' rooms."

He hesitated a moment then asked, "Cards from car salesmen?"

"From men we've gone out with." When he remained silent, she took the plunge and added, "On dates."

She heard him cursing beneath his breath before he came back. "And you want me to respond to that how?"

She scooted farther up onto the bed, settling into her pillows. If she was in for a penny, she might as well go for the pound, she mused, before blurting, "We also write notes. On the backs of the cards."

"What? You rate the guy or something?" he asked, a definite edge to his voice.

She found herself smiling. "Not rate, no. More like review."

"Sharing the lowdown on the losers, huh?"

"Oh, no," she hurried to say. "We don't share anything about losers. Only about good guys. Ones who might not have worked for us, but might for one of the other women."

"Thanks." He grumbled beneath his breath. "I'm feeling really special now."

She grinned, imagining the frown he must be wearing. God, he had always made her feel good, no matter what she was facing. "You should. Someone thought you were hell on wheels in bed."

He cleared his throat. "I'll be sure to put that on my résumé."

He would joke about it, of course, instead of volunteering a name. God, but she was pathetic, as if she really needed to know. His love life was not her concern. "The more references the better, I suppose."

"Are you fishing, Milla?"

"Of course not," she lied, pathetic, pathetic, pathetic. "It's none of my business who you've dated."

"Or who I've slept with."

She nodded, knowing he couldn't see her. "Yeah. That, too."

"But you still want to know, don't you?"

He was making it way too easy to say yes. To act like a schoolgirl with a crush and a gossip-empty well. A mature adult understood the intimate nature of what went on between men and women.

So why did the thought of another woman knowing Rennie's body the way she did cause such an incredible tightness in her chest?

She needed therapy. That's all there was to it.

"No. I don't." She really was trying to be the bigger woman—a hard task when she felt so very small.

"Good," he said after several interminable seconds, his voice softer now. "You not wanting to know saves me from telling you that the good times I've had have been just that. Nothing but fun. Nothing permanent."

"So you've never been in love?" she asked before thinking about what she was asking, the position she was putting him in, the hurt she was setting herself up to suffer.

He was quiet for the longest time, coming back to say, "I was once, yeah. It didn't…work out."

"I'm sorry." If he only knew how very sorry she was. How many things she wanted to take back.

"Hey," he said, and she imagined a shrug. "Sometimes we just don't have what it takes to figure things out. Or we wait too long to make them right."

Because we're too young? she wanted to ask. She was certain that he was talking about what they'd had, yet she was too afraid of the truth to ask. "I see a lot of clients like that at work. Repeat offenders."

"Good for the bottom line, though, yes? Making a tidy profit off the losers who can't tell a good thing from a hole in the ground?"

Is that what he really thought? Or was he baiting her for some reason? "At MatchMeUp we arrange for people to meet and see how they fit. What looks good on paper doesn't always translate so well to real life."

He gave a mocking sort of snort in response. "And here I thought those long walks on the beach were all it took to cement a relationship."

"You are a cynical man, Rennie Bergen."

"I quit believing in happy endings a long time ago, Milla. I think you know when. And I think you know why."

She might be sorry for what had happened, but she was not going to shoulder all the blame. "Oh, so this lousy loser life you lead is now my fault?"

"Lousy loser. That coming from the woman who's surrounded herself with bland?"

Neither spoke after that, letting the silence between them linger and take on a life of its own. Yet neither seemed to want to end the call. And that need to stay connected said more about their unsettled past than her colorless world or his cynicism.

"I was just noticing that," she finally said, clearing her throat that was clogged with emotion. "I was trying to decide what to wear this weekend, and hadn't realized how much of my wardrobe is black."

"Remind me where it is we're going," he said.

She gave him the name of the restaurant adding, "It's fairly…high-brow."

"Whatever. Just wear something I can get you out of without a lot of work."

His words thrilled her; she hated that they did, loved that they did, hated, loved, she was going insane. "Assuming a lot, aren't you?"

"I'm not assuming anything. I'm looking forward to the obvious."

"And what obvious would that be?" she asked, her blood near boiling.

"Ever tossed a burning match into a pool of gasoline?"

"Not lately."

"What about Friday night? In your kitchen? That's how we mix, Milla. Like fire and gasoline."

"I was thinking we were more like oil and water."

Rennie laughed, a deep seductive invitation to prove him wrong. "Don't tell me you're not thinking about sleeping with me right now."

"About sleeping with you in the past? Sure," she said, her voice breaking. "It's crossed my mind a time or two."

"Not the past. Now. Right now. This very moment."

The way he seduced her was so unfair. He didn't have to be in the same room. She didn't have to look into his eyes, run her hands over his body.

She didn't even have to feel the touch of his hands on hers. All it took was his voice and her memories to set her on fire. A lit match and gasoline, just like he'd said.

"Maybe," she finally said. Then she admitted the truth. "Okay, yes. I'm thinking about you."

"What about me?"

"About sleeping with you."

"Sleeping with me, or having sex with me?"

"The latter," she said, squeezing her thighs together. "No sleeping involved."

"Where are you? Right now?"

"In my bedroom. Trying on clothes like I told you."

"Are you undressed?"

"No…" she hedged. "I've got on what will best show off whatever I decide to wear over it."

He gave a growling sort of laugh. "What's that supposed to mean?"

"Panty lines are never pretty. I'm wearing a thong."

"What else?"

"A bra that claims to have the magical ability to make the most of my assets."

"There's nothing wrong with your assets."

She couldn't help it. "Sure you didn't mean 'what assets'?"

He groaned in her ear. "It's hard to have phone sex with you complaining."

She laughed. "I wasn't aware we were having phone sex."

"It's not for lack of trying on my part."

"I was also unaware that you were so handy with fire and gasoline metaphors," she said, tucking her toes beneath the patchwork quilt folded on the foot of her bed.

"There's a lot you don't know about me."

It was time for a change of subject. Sex they'd always have. "So, tell me something that you want me to know."

"You know everything you need to know already."

"I didn't know about the metaphor thing."

"And you could have gone the rest of your life without finding out."

"So why did the papers you wrote for English lit suck so badly?"

"Because I didn't give a crap about English lit?"

She shook her head. "Nope. Don't buy it. You cared about everything in school because you wanted your degree for your family."

"I wrote crap papers so you'd have to fix them."

She sat up straight. "What?"

"I didn't really need a tutor, you know. But when Derek suggested it so I wouldn't stress over flunking out…"

Her blood pressure began to rise. "You were never on the verge of getting kicked out?"

"Nope."

"So I wasted all that time tutoring you instead of focusing on my own work?"

"It wasn't a waste."

"Easy for you to say," she grumbled, though she really wasn't mad. She couldn't be.

"C'mon, Milla. Admit it. That time we spent together without hiding or sneaking around was pretty damn good."

The hiding and sneaking wasn't so bad, either. "Maybe. But that doesn't excuse you for lying to me."

This time his cynical laugh was tinged with sarcasm. "We lied to everyone else, why not each other? And don't tell me you never lied to me."

Did he know about her parents? How Derek had been their choice of son-in-law? She swallowed hard, drew her knees to her chest. "What if we make a deal? Right here and now."

"I'm not a big fan of deals."

"Too bad. You make this one, or you never see me again."

"I know where you live."

"I'll move," she lied.

"I know where you work."

"I'll transfer," she lied.

"You can't not see me again. You need a date for Friday," he reminded her.

"I have a little black book filled with names."

"What's the deal?"

She loved it when he gave in. "From now on, from this very moment, we never lie to each other again."

"Sounds like an admission of guilt, to me."

"Deal or no deal?"

"Now it sounds like a TV show."

"Rennie? I'm going to hang up on you in about five seconds...four, three, two—"

"Yeah, yeah, all right. No more lies."

"Even little white ones."

"Cross my heart and hope to get you naked."

"You're hopeless, you know that?"

"So I've been told."

"By who?"

"Uh-huh. Just because I'm bound not to lie doesn't mean I'm bound to tell you the truth."

"Fine."

"But, since I have agreed to your deal..."

"Yes?"

"I want to hear more about that bra you're wearing," he said, and she dissolved into laughter.

9

INSTEAD OF SHOPPING for something colorful to wear, Milla spent the rest of the week inordinately busy at work and ended up settling for basic black on Friday.

Black was always in, always appropriate. She wasn't happy that she'd somehow let it take over her closet, but at least she wouldn't have to worry about evening wear anytime soon.

And if Rennie didn't like it, well, she wasn't dressing for Rennie. Okay, she was, and her Wednesday night closet raid easily outed her lie.

But since they'd only agreed not to lie to each other, she had every right to go on lying to herself. Though she really did need to stop, honesty being the best policy and all, and avoiding the truth getting her nowhere and getting her there fast.

Tonight she'd arranged to meet him at the rumored-to-be-wildly romantic restaurant she was scheduled to review instead of having him pick her up. She didn't want to risk another kitchen table sex incident, and knew full well that clothes were likely to go flying everywhere the next time they found themselves alone.

The issue with sex on the kitchen table—or any-where for that matter—wasn't about enjoyment or the lack thereof. It was simply that she didn't need to be having sex with Rennie, she reminded herself as she parked her car.

Doing so in the past had resulted in too much heart-ache, heartbreak, and too many ruined lives. Yes, they were older, but obviously they were no wiser, judging by the way the topic of sex continued to come up be-tween them.

It was almost as if their connection was an addic-tion rather than any sort of temporary infatuation. Or an infatuation that was more permanent, she mused, checking her hair and her lipstick before opening the car door. Here it was six years since graduation, and she still couldn't get him out of her mind.

She climbed from her car, smoothed down her skirt and hit the remote lock. If she didn't know better, she might wonder if their thing in college had been more than a back alley affair. If she hadn't actually fallen in love with him then. If she wasn't still in love with him now.

The very real possibility that she was sent her reel-ing, and she caught herself against the hood of her car when she stumbled. She could not possibly have fallen in love with Rennie Bergen. Not then when he'd been a distraction she'd desperately needed, and certainly not now.

She was smart. She was successful. She managed her own portfolio and owned her own home. She would never confuse a past indiscretion or a current infatuation with an emotion as consuming and vital as love— unless she'd been lying to herself all this time.

She slowed as she caught sight of Rennie waiting outside of the restaurant door. He wore a dark suit, either black or navy, an ivory dress shirt, designer tie and Italian leather loafers. He'd tamed back his hair but had done nothing with the shadow of his beard.

He stood on the sidewalk, his hands in his pants' pockets, the tails of his coat flaring behind him. He was tall, his shoulders broad, his waist and hips deliciously lean. The stubble on his face defined the hard line of his jaw, and his dark brown eyes were piercing.

She wanted to eat him up.

She wanted to love him until the day she died.

She wanted to turn around and go home, and shove her past into the past where it belonged.

She didn't want to feel as if the rest of her life hinged on tonight.

But she stayed the course, her heart racing, her fingers shaking, her stomach in knots, and told herself to stop being so overdramatic. This was a date. A date that was also her job. And it was the job part that was dragging her down. She didn't want to have to soak up the atmosphere, or critique the service, or worry about finding out where the chef bought his heirloom tomatoes.

She wanted tonight to be about her and Rennie.

"Hey," she said at last, snagging his attention.

He turned toward her, taking her in from head to toe, the heat in his eyes simmering, the look he gave her appreciative, bone-melting…and possessive. He pulled his hands from his pockets and reached out.

"You look stunning," he said, his fingers warm and demanding when they closed around hers.

It never failed to amaze her the difference in their sizes. He made her feel smaller than she really was, while he was so much larger than life. All she could think of to say was, "Thank you."

He continued to stare, his nostrils flaring. "Forget I ever complained about you lacking color. You do really good things to black."

She felt herself beaming. "Are you sure it's not black doing really good things to me?"

"No way," he said, then leaned in to whisper, "But now I really want to know what you're wearing underneath it."

"That would be *not* wearing," she whispered seductively, giving him a wink before pulling him groaning toward the restaurant door.

"You are a cruel woman, Milla Page. Don't think I won't pay you back." That was all he got out before they stepped through the door, but he squeezed her hand to let her know he meant it.

Milla gave the hostess her name and then she and Rennie followed the young woman through what was essentially a rabbit warren. Individual alcoves sat off both sides of the winding hallway that went up three steps here, down two steps there, even making a turn through the kitchen where a table was tucked in one corner. For gastronomics?

Milla couldn't help but be swept up in the ambience. The intimacy of the surroundings promoted a soft romanticism she couldn't resist. She understood why the restaurant had made it onto the list of locations the home office had assigned for review. She felt like Alice tumbling through a wonderland of dreamy possibilities.

Like each of the other recesses, the one to which the hostess led them had a name. This one was "The Vineyard," and Milla could see why. The small circular table was draped with merlot-covered linen, a hue that complimented the deep red and burgundy paisley that covered the half-moon banquette. She made a mental note to find out more about the designer.

Milla slid in on one side. Rennie slid in on the other. The hostess presented them with a menu and told them to expect the sommelier shortly to discuss their choices of wine, their specialty being vintages from Napa.

Once the other woman left, Milla glanced around the small enclosed space, ignoring Rennie's snort before he said, "I feel like I'm sitting inside an eggplant."

She glanced over. "Have you ever cut open an eggplant? It's aubergine on the outside. The inside is a pale yellow."

"Okay, then. An inside-out eggplant."

"I think it's cozy," she said, settling back into the banquette's plush seat. The lamp hanging low over the table cast a soft warm glow, and the paper on the surrounding walls depicted an arbor of vines heavy with grapes.

Rennie snorted. "Only if your idea of cozy is to embrace your inner fruit."

Milla glanced from the wine rack overhead to her dinner partner. Her date. Mr. Cynicism himself. "What is wrong with you? Inner fruit."

The sommelier arrived then and before Milla could say a word, Rennie took over, discussing wines as if he'd been a vintner all of his life.

She listened in awe as the two men talked about body, sugar, color and flavor, nodding when Rennie asked for her approval on his selection.

She waited until the sommelier had disappeared into the warren before speaking. "Wow. I'm impressed."

He shook out his napkin, spread it over his lap. "Didn't think an auto mechanic had it in him, did you?"

"I'm not a snob, Rennie," she said, tucking her purse close to her hip as she reached for her napkin, too. "I just didn't know you were into wines."

"Wine, women, metaphor and most recently, song," he said as the sommelier returned and poured. Once he'd gone, Rennie continued. "I went to Austin on business in May and was introduced to a lot of local musicians. I've been on an Alejandro Escovedo kick lately."

She ignored his cultural repertoire and latched on to something else he'd said. "Introduced to the musicians, or just to their work?"

"Some of one, a little of the other."

"What kind of business would take you halfway across the country?"

"I was looking for a specific car."

"And you had to go to Texas to find it?"

He shrugged. "I was working on a modification to

an old Studebaker. There aren't a lot of those to be had, so I had to go there to check it out."

She knew nothing about cars so she didn't respond, but she had the feeling she was missing something big here. "You know, it's hard to believe you're the same Rennie Bergen that I used to know. So much about you has changed."

His eyes shone brightly beneath his dark brows. "Did you expect me to stay twenty-four forever?"

"It's not that, the age thing. It's not even about maturing and growing up—"

"I refuse to grow up," he said after cutting her off. "And I refuse to mature. Why let kids have all the fun when they're too young to know how good they've got it?"

Maybe that was it. His attitude. When she'd known him in college he'd been so serious and intense. But now, even though he seemed harder and was definitely more cynical, he appeared to be enjoying himself.

"So, what have you done lately that's been fun?"

He raised a brow. "Besides cooking on your kitchen table?"

No sex. No sex talk. A change of subject. "Do you cook?"

"Food?"

"Yes, food. You've turned into a connoisseur of wine, women, metaphor and song. I would think food would be an obvious addition to your passions."

He shook his head. "My passion is cars. The rest just get me through the day."

Hmm. She wasn't sure how she felt about being just another distraction. "I guess that means you won't be inviting me up for a home-cooked meal anytime soon."

He considered her a moment as if weighing what he wanted to say, surprising her by asking, "Why don't you come for Thanksgiving?"

"What?" Was he kidding?

"Sure. Why not?" He sat back, settling comfortably. "It's a huge event at our house."

"I know. You used to talk about it every year." She'd been so envious when he had.

"Then come." He waved one hand, an inviting gesture. "My mother would love to see you again."

"I don't know." The thought of facing his parents after her past with their son… "What do they know about us? About everything?"

He shrugged, toyed with the base of his wineglass. "Not much. Just that I took off after graduation."

"Do they know why?" she asked, though she hated to.

"Sure." He lifted his glass and emptied it in one swallow. "That I got my heart broken and needed the time alone to get over it."

"Your heart broke—" She looked away, blinked hard, thankful that their server arrived to take their dinner order. She chose a simple pasta primavera, Rennie went for a steak.

The sommelier followed on the server's heels to refill their wineglasses, then they were once again on their own. Stuck with each other in the cozy warmth of the inside-out eggplant.

She couldn't have broken his heart. She didn't believe it for a minute. His heart had never been involved. They'd never talked of their feelings. She'd certainly never admitted to hers. And yet...

Her eyes were still damp when she sighed. "I never wanted anyone to get hurt."

"My eyes were open, Milla. I knew what I was doing."

"I wish I had. I was so stupid. I thought somehow we'd be okay." *That we'd end up together,* she stopped herself from adding.

Rennie wasn't wearing her same rose-colored glasses. "Hard to make it happen with Derek in the picture."

She reached again for her wineglass. "You don't understand about Derek."

"What's to understand? You were dating him, sleeping with him."

Here goes nothing...or everything. "I was supposed to marry him."

He bit off a curse. "Sorry for fouling that up."

She shook her head. "No. I mean, it was a thing our parents had arranged. A business deal."

"That's archaic."

The way she'd described it, yeah. She could see how it looked. "I don't mean it was an arranged marriage."

"Then what?"

She might as well start at the beginning, tell him everything, be honest at last. "Derek and I knew each other in high school."

"I know that part," he barked.

Her gaze shot to his. "Well, if you'll quit interrupting, I'll tell you the rest."

He nodded, reached for his wine. Their server arrived with their salads, and Milla waited until the pepper and parmesan had been ground and grated before she explained anything more.

She picked up her salad fork; she wasn't hungry, just wanted something to do with her hands. "I didn't just know Derek. Our parents were friends, too. They did all the things couples who are members of the same country club and social set do. Golf, tennis, dinner parties. Even sailing and fund-raising."

"My folks played bingo and rounded up the neighborhood for block party barbecues," Rennie said, his sarcasm heavy.

Even so, she wasn't going to let him hijack her tale. He could listen or he could be pissy. She didn't want to have to talk about this more than once.

She waited until he'd raised his gaze to hers to respond. "If you're going to turn this into a social commentary, I'm done."

"I'm all ears," he said, stabbing his salad. "Entertain me."

"Fine," she said, then took a deep breath. "Derek and I were drafted into helping out with the parents' various projects. We became…close. We started dating. The parents joked about eventually becoming in-laws. And then when Derek and I stayed together in college, they got serious."

"About the two of you getting serious?"

She could tell by his tone that he was finally paying attention. "No, about Derek's father absorbing my father's business into his own, and their becoming partners."

Rennie frowned down at his salad. "What happened?"

"The graduation party."

"Wait a minute." He gestured with his fork. "You mean the fact that you and I were screwing around busted up a merger? Are your fathers Donald and Daffy Duck? Why in the hell would two adults let their kids' sex lives screw up a business deal?"

Her sentiments exactly. She'd lived through it all and still couldn't get a handle on her father's or Dick Randall's way of thinking. "You've got to remember that Derek and I were both only children. Spoiled only children. The sun around which our parents' worlds revolved."

Rennie sat back while their food was placed on the table and their barely touched salads taken away. Once their server was gone, Rennie stared at her, studying her, finally saying, "So Daffy and Donald went at it from ten paces."

It sounded so ridiculous that she wanted to laugh. "Something like that."

"What happened?"

"Nothing. The deal fell through. My father had stupidly borrowed heavily against the anticipated income."

"He lost his shirt."

She nodded. "My mother went into a horrible depression. I did what I could…." She didn't really want to give him the details of her trust fund. "But we don't speak anymore."

Rennie leaned forward then, braced his elbows on the edge of the table, hung his head between his hands. "And I took off, leaving you to deal with all that."

"You didn't know." She reached over and squeezed his forearm. "I didn't want you to know."

"I would have stayed if you'd told me, Milla." He lifted his head, met her gaze, her eyes wide with emotion. "If I'd stayed, we might've had a shot—"

She placed her fingers over his mouth, her heart aching. "Don't. I've second-guessed everything that happened. I've done it enough for both of us. I've moved on, and you certainly don't need to move back. That's one thing I'd never be able to forgive myself for. If by looking you up again for selfish reasons, I've ended up ruining your life."

He covered her hand on his arm, toyed with her fingers. "Why did you look me up?"

"Curiosity," she said, and tried to pull away.

He held her tight. "You wanted to see what I'd made of myself?"

She turned her hand over, teased his palm with her nails. "Last time we talked you told me you were off to make a million."

"Money-grubbing wench," he said, and groaned, capturing her flirting fingers.

She moved closer, her blood sizzling, and breathed him in. "I wasn't curious about your money. I told you. It was your business card."

"Right. And that thing about me being hell on wheels in bed." He paused, thought a moment, then went on. "So I have curiosity and jealousy to thank for you finally getting around to looking me up?"

She didn't want to admit to the jealousy, though it was better than trying to explain the whole truth of the feelings that had rushed through her upon seeing his name.

Still, she felt as if they were finally getting somewhere, being honest, opening up about things they should have never waited so long to talk about.

And so she told him the truth. "If your ego needs the stroke, then sure. I'll admit it."

"Are you about done there?" he asked, looking at her half-eaten meal.

She had planned on ordering dessert to complete her review, but… Eyes narrowed and blood humming, she asked, "Why? Are you ready to go?"

"Yeah. I'll follow you home."

"No dessert?"

"It can wait. I've got something other than my ego needing to be stroked," he said, and she laughed feeling exactly the same.

10

FRIDAY NIGHT found Hector working late alone—a situation that wasn't uncommon. He knew overtime didn't make a lot of sense money-wise since he was a salaried employee.

Week in and week out his paycheck was the same, no matter how many hours he put in. He made good money, so the time spent wasn't about making more.

Sometimes he just stayed longer than he had to because he didn't have a reason to go home and felt working made for a better use of those hours.

Then there were times like tonight when he was feeling the downside of living alone, and keeping busy kept the depression from settling too deep.

He didn't get lonely often. He volunteered with a local Latino immigrant shelter. He worked out at the gym. He partied with his close friends. He watched ball games and fights with his neighbors.

But he did miss his family a lot, and the distance between San Francisco and El Salvador sometimes seemed too far to get over. At least he was doing right by his parents and siblings, sending most of his money home. Rennie was the only one who knew that's what he did.

Hector liked it that way. He didn't want to hear what a good son he was when guilt ate at him constantly because he hadn't been home to visit in thirteen years.

When he'd first come to work for Bergen Motors, he'd chosen to send his money home instead of spending it to travel. Now that he worked for Rennie and "Hell on Wheels," he could afford to do both, but he didn't—for reasons he kept to himself.

He did call. And he'd fixed up his folks with a satellite dish for phone, Internet and television to keep them in touch. Each episode of "Hell on Wheels" was a huge event where the entire village gathered to see him.

The thing was, he wanted to be able to go home and be himself, not the Prieto's cable TV star son. He didn't like that his family saw him as being different now because he was living the American dream.

He didn't like how they expected him to do things they couldn't. How they didn't understand when he failed—

"Hector?"

He backed out from under the hood of the Studebaker Rennie had brought up from Austin and glanced around the body of the car.

Angie was walking toward him, her flowery skirt swinging around her knees with each step. Wisps of hair had escaped the coil at her neck and clung to her skin.

He looked away, grabbed a shop rag from his pocket and wiped his hands. "Ang. What are you doing here?"

"Coming to ask you the same thing. I left a package I'd picked up for my mamma under my desk and saw your truck when I came back for it." She stopped at the back end of the Studebaker, cocked her hip to one side and crossed her arms over her chest. "Why are you still working?"

He shrugged, toying with the shop rag. "Didn't have any plans, and wasn't in the mood to go home."

"And whose fault is that?" she asked, all bossy like.

One corner of his mouth twisted upward. "My personal assistant's for not booking me for tonight, and my interior designer's for not giving the place a homey feel?"

For the longest time, she stared at him without saying a word. He didn't know her well enough to figure out what she was thinking, but with Angie being as prickly as she was, he was pretty sure he was about to find out.

He wasn't wrong.

"What in the world are you talking about?" she asked, her hands going to her hips. "A personal assistant and an interior designer?"

"It was supposed to be funny." He said that instead of telling her how cute she was when she got all uppity, and how he was having a hard time keeping his hands to himself.

"Humph. It sounded more like you were trying to show off what you've been doing with all the money Rennie's show pays you," she said, gesturing sharply with one hand, her pink nails flashing.

That made him want to laugh even more than it made him want to tell her about his family in El Salvador. "I'm afraid you'd have to go to Central America to see what I've been doing with my money."

"What? You're running a coffee plantation there?"

"Not a plantation. A village."

"You don't say," she said, and pursed her lips. "So if you've got this big place…what? In the mountains? On the coast? Why don't you ever go visit? I don't think you've taken a vacation since I started working here." She huffed, added, "Maybe if you did you'd be in a better mood."

Hector headed to the worktable and the carburetor he had torn apart, determined to put a lid on this conversation before he actually told Angie things he didn't want her to know. "I wouldn't know what to do on a vacation. I like to keep busy."

Angie followed him across the garage, her heels clacking against the concrete floor. "You can keep busy on a vacation. You don't have to sleep till noon and spend the rest of the day at the hotel pool ordering umbrella drinks."

He found himself grinning. "Is that what you do on vacation?"

She sighed heavily, settling in as if she had nothing else to do. "I never have, but I wouldn't turn down the chance if someone handed it to me."

He reached for a socket and a wrench. "I'd probably end up in the pool house tuning up the pump motor."

She watched silently for several seconds as he worked, the only sound that of his tools and his breathing, until she asked, "Do you like working with your hands, or is it just what you're best at?"

"A little bit of both, I guess." He'd never really thought about it. "I probably like it because being good at it means I don't get bored or frustrated."

"I get both at the front desk sometimes," she admitted. "All those calls and messages, and it hardly takes half a brain to do any of it."

He glanced over, surprised she didn't seem to realize how good she was at her job. "You do a lot more than that. And you do that better than anyone who's worked the switchboard in years."

"Really?"

She always seemed so confident, he'd never thought she might be questioning her own performance. Or if anyone noticed the effort she made.

He nodded, went back to work. "Seriously. The lady before you couldn't handle even two calls at a time. Rennie's mom had to come fill in until they hired you."

"I met Mrs. Bergen. She's the one who interviewed me." Angie picked up a socket, tapped it against the table. "It's funny because I didn't know anything about the show then. I mean, that it's connected to Bergen Motors."

"That's been Rennie's doing. He didn't want his folks to have to deal with the media and fans and stuff."

"But I'd think knowing Bergen Motors was the home of "Hell on Wheels" would be good for sales."

"Maybe. I dunno. It was what Rennie worked out with his dad. I think his dad wanted the Bergen Motors rep to stand on its own, you know? Not have the business's success be tied into the show."

"Well, I'm no business tycoon, but I say who cares where the money comes from as long as it's coming in."

Hector shrugged. "Things are working, so I guess they know what they're doing."

"I suppose. I just know that I'd take every advantage to build up a business I owned."

"Yeah, but making the connection between Rennie and Bergen Motors might have backfired."

"How so?" she asked, returning the socket to its tray.

"Too much business. More than the family could handle without expanding."

"Is expanding a bad thing?"

"Depends, I guess. Rennie says his folks want to retire soon. I can't see them wanting to take on more work if that's the case."

"Even if there's more income?"

Hector pushed aside the parts and the tools, knowing he wouldn't be getting anything else done today and not caring at all. "Life isn't all about money, Ang."

"Easy for you to say, Mr. Moneybags, Lord of the Village."

Hector laughed. "That's the last·thing you'd be calling me if you saw how I lived."

Less than a second passed before she pounced. "How do you live?"

"I've got a bed in the bedroom," he began, wondering what she was fishing for because he'd be glad to tell her straight out that he wasn't a good catch. "I've got a couch, a coffee table and a TV in the living room. That's it."

Angie frowned. "Just one bedroom?"

"Yep."

"No dining room?"

"Nope. Hardwood floors, white walls, nice Italian tile in the kitchen."

She considered what he'd told her then said, "So you've got a nice place, you just haven't furnished it."

"It's furnished," he said with a laugh, watching her expression shift from one emotion to another as she tried to figure out exactly who he was.

Her eyes narrowed. "A bed, a couch, a coffee table and a television is not furnished, Hector."

He shrugged, headed back toward the car. "It's all I need."

"No wonder you're working late if that's all that's waiting for you at home," she called from behind him.

"It's not so bad," he said, even though he'd been thinking pretty much the same thing.

Her heels struck the concrete floor with a new determination. "And I'm sure you eat on the coffee table in front of the TV."

"That, or over the kitchen sink while looking out the window."

"That's terrible."

He had to tease her. "Did I mention that I drink my milk and my OJ straight from the carton?"

She closed her eyes and shuddered as if she could not imagine anyone being that uncouth. And when she looked at him again, she surprised him by asking, "What are you doing tomorrow?"

He hadn't really thought about it. More of the boring same nothing at home. Or else working. He made his choice. "Working."

Her brows went up. "Rennie said? Or you're just doing it."

"Rennie may be around. I don't know."

"You work till noon. Then I'll come by and we'll go shopping." She paused, frowned, added, "You have money for shopping, don't you?"

He had some, but… "Shopping for what?"

"You need art. A painting or something." She gestured widely. "And a lamp. Do you have a lamp?"

He just used the light from the ceiling fixture most of the time. "No."

"A floor lamp then, since you don't have tables. Something to show off the art."

"If you say so."

"I do." She blew out a heavy breath as if she'd tired herself out solving a pressing problem. "I'm not saying you need to clutter up the place. My mamma is the perfect example of overkill. But a painting or a print will give your place personality. And going home won't be so hard to do."

She was a bossy little thing, but he couldn't deny that she might be right. His apartment had always been a place to stay. Turning it into a home…

He'd grown up expecting to have the barest necessities and no more. He supposed he was still thinking like a kid lucky enough to have shoes with no holes instead of like a kid who could afford more than one pair.

Maybe it was time he enjoyed a little bit more of what he had instead of feeling guilty about it. He liked the way Angie knew what he needed better than he did.

And so he said, "Okay, then. I'll see you at noon."

11

SHE LET HIM COME home with her. Rennie couldn't believe it. He'd been such a prick over dinner...yet Milla had invited him up the stairs with a smile.

He deserved to be shot. Castrated. Strung up by his balls until his whole body turned blue. Instead he was going to have the pleasure of making love to a woman he couldn't get out of his mind.

This was date number two out of the three they'd arranged, discussing the final one as they'd walked to their cars. He was already looking ahead to the last date. Not because their time together would be over, but because he was determined that it wouldn't.

He was not going to let her walk out of his life after next weekend. Not when they'd come this far and been given this chance after so much time apart.

The agreement they'd made to be honest was a very good beginning. That phone call had been something, the things she'd told him. He loved how she didn't let him get to her; no matter how deep he dug, she climbed right out of his trap—and tossed the dirt back down on his head.

Then there were the revelations she'd made tonight during dinner… He was still thinking about punching the people who'd given her so much grief. What kind of family used its members like pawns? But he was also battling the urge to kick his own ass.

It had been tunnel vision that had kept him from seeing that he should have stuck around. That she'd needed him to stick around. He'd been too focused on her betrayal at the party, on her accusation that he'd meant nothing to her, to see the truth. Too caught up in believing that he never had to tell her.

What a big fat cluster bomb of miscommunication. And even as he acknowledged that truth, he knew he wasn't ready to tell her everything about who he was now. He wasn't worried about her looking at him with dollar signs in her eyes. But he sure didn't want her looking at him as if he wasn't the same man she'd once known.

Maybe that hesitation had to do with his sense of her being broken…and wanting to know even more about her before sharing more of himself. He really wasn't sure and, right now, he really didn't care.

Tonight was a definite case of so far, so good that he didn't want to screw up. And now that they'd reached her landing—the climb and his thoughts helping to tame the beast it had been hard to rein in when sitting so close in the eggplant, smelling her, watching her, touching her when she had let him…

"Would you like coffee?" she asked, pushing the door open and pulling her keys from the lock. "More wine? Something stronger?"

He waited for her to shut the door, toss her purse and her keys on the secretary before answering. He wanted her full attention. He didn't want her thinking about drinks—only about him.

When she turned and looked up, having kicked off her shoes and halfway through removing the tiny studs from her ears, her smile grew inquisitive. "What's wrong?"

He shook his head. Nothing was wrong. He just didn't want to talk. They'd talked all night. They'd talked for what seemed like hours on Wednesday. Talking took them to places they needed to go. Right now, however, he didn't want to go anywhere but to her bed.

He held out his hand. She glanced down, but didn't take it. Not until her gaze had returned to his and she saw his intent. Only then did she curl the tips of her fingers over the tips of his and take a step down the hall.

He went with her silently, itching to slide the zipper of her dress from her nape to the small of her back. He wanted to bare her skin slowly, to learn for himself exactly what she had on underneath, if she was as naked as he'd imagined her to be, as scantily covered as she'd teased him.

She left the light off when they entered the bedroom. He didn't mind. The sheer gauze panels over the room's single window let in enough from the moon and the street for him to see what he wanted.

She stopped at the foot of the bed and, still holding his hand, turned into the curve of his arm. She brought their laced fingers to rest behind her back, and he pulled her flush against him.

"Look at me, Milla," he finally said, breaking the silence, his voice not as steady as he'd hoped.

It took her a moment to respond, but she finally lifted her chin, her gaze crawling slowly from his chest to his face, her eyes wide and clear and hungry.

He swallowed against the emotion he saw shimmering there. It took him back in time…. "I'm sorry I didn't stick around after graduation. That I wasn't there for you during all the crap that went down."

"Oh, Rennie. You couldn't have known it would happen. Even I didn't know it would happen." She released his hand, wrapped her arms around his neck. Her mouth formed a humorless grin. "It was pretty crushing, having to accept that my parents' approval of Derek hinged on more than him being a nice guy."

Rennie didn't want to talk about her parents, and he sure didn't want to talk about another man. What he wanted was to feel her bare body lift up to meet his. He set both of his hands at her waist, slid them higher until his thumbs brushed the lower swell of her breasts and she shivered. "So you like nice guys?"

This time her grin was the perfect tease. "They have their uses."

He raised a brow. "You like not-so-nice-guys better?"

"I'm not sure I know any. But I have heard rumors…."

He leaned down, nuzzled her neck beneath her ear, filled himself with her spicy, flowery scent and whispered, "Nasty rumors?"

She shivered, nodded. "Uh-huh."

"Care to share?"

"Well, some of the girls at the office—"

"The ones with the business cards?"

She laughed softly. "Those, yes, among others. They told me—"

"What?" he pressed, because he was impatient beyond belief.

"That the not-so-nice-guys are better kissers."

"That so?" he asked, and nipped her earlobe, loving the soft fall of her hair against his cheek.

"Like I said," she murmured a minute or two later. "I'm not sure I've met any to know."

He growled as he covered her breasts with his hands. "Oh, you've met at least one."

"I thought you might say that."

"Should we test this kissing theory?"

"I'm up for anything," she said as he leaned back to look into her eyes.

He gave her his biggest, baddest grin. "I was hoping you'd say that."

Her only response was to pull his mouth down to hers. The hunger he'd seen in her eyes wasn't the half of it. She tugged his coat off his shoulders, her lips catching his as he shrugged out of the jacket and pulled loose his tie.

She moved to tackle his buttons and didn't stop until she'd bared his chest, her mouth drifting lower to explore his skin. She sprinkled kisses down his neck, and her hands followed, kneading and rubbing until he groaned from the ground up.

"This is no way to conduct a kissing experiment." He needed her to slow down or else this entire night would be one big backfire.

She found his nipple, circled it with her tongue. "I'm trying the one-sided, selfish approach."

"And you're doing a damn fine job." He grabbed her by the shoulders and set her away. "But this would be a hell of a lot more fun if you'd let me in on the action."

When she pouted, he forcefully turned her around, finally getting his hands on her zipper and sliding it down. Once he'd opened her dress as far as he could, she wiggled and the fabric puddled on the floor at her feet.

He hissed back a breath, instantly growing hard and wanting to touch her everywhere at once, settling for pulling her tightly against him and wrapping his arms around her waist. Her skin was smooth like glass, cool like the night breeze.

He slid his hands up to cup her breasts, holding their slight weight tenderly. Milla wasn't so tender at all. She reached back, seizing the fabric of his pockets to keep him still, and doing a mean bump and grind against the swelling in his groin.

He could have taken her right then and there. Bent her over the bed and shoved into her from behind. He was that hard, that ready. But getting off that way wasn't enough, not this time. And so he kissed her neck, holding her hands in his, sliding their joined fingers beneath the elastic of her thong and into her warm, wet folds.

She moaned and shuddered. He felt it along her

spine where he pressed her close, felt it rattle her ribs where he held her. He felt it with his hand questing between her legs, and wondered if she felt it, too.

He slipped their fingers lower, making a V around her clit and squeezing with his knuckles, deepening the touch and finding her opening, pushing both of their index fingers inside.

She cried out. She whimpered. She contracted the muscles of her sex and squeezed. "Rennie, please. I need more. I need you."

He needed her just as much, and he needed her now. Later he'd take his time. Later, again and again…

He let her go while he stripped off his pants, watching her make quick work of her thong and crawl backward onto the bed. He followed, slipping on a condom, grabbing hold of his shaft, and guiding his cock into place.

He entered her more roughly than he'd intended, and she came up off the bed, her hips arching, her back bowing. After that, he tendered his movements, loving her slowly, holding her wrists pinned above her head while he ground his hips against hers.

It didn't take either one of them long. So much had built up between them, desire and tension warring with reserve and control, the physical pleasure winning in the end. Milla grew still, then burst and cried out, and her orgasm pulled his free.

He pumped harder, faster, shoved into her deeper, gave her everything he had until he felt as if he'd died. It took him forever to come down, and when he did, minutes later, still lying on top of her, their bodies joined, he was pretty damn sure that's what had happened. That after all these years of loving her, Milla had finally done him in.

"IF I'D KNOWN YOU were going to be so quick on the draw, I'd have kissed you good night on the stairs and gone to bed with a book," Milla said, plucking at the hair in the center of Rennie's chest.

He captured her hand, held her still. "This from the woman who nearly ruined a perfectly good shirt ripping it off."

She snorted. "I did not rip it. I didn't even tear off a single button."

"But you did come first."

"What does that have to do with anything?"

"I figured since you got yours, it was time for me to get mine."

"Hmm. Well, I will give you credit for not packing up your toys and going home."

"Oh, I never cut out on a play date when I'm having fun."

"Are you?" she asked softly, looking down to where he lay beneath her, his cock once again hard where it filled her. "Having fun?"

Rennie frowned, his dark brows slashing into a V. "What kind of question is that?"

"The same kind I always ask. One I want you to answer." The man was determined to make her nuts.

He slid his hands up her thighs where she straddled

him and squeezed. "Milla, I've always had fun being with you."

"In bed."

"With *you*. Always."

"Always." She didn't want things to get sticky. She didn't want to push. "Is that like every time? Or is that like forever?"

"Are you looking for forever?"

"Honestly? I don't know if I'm ready."

"What do you know?"

"I know I don't want you to disappear from my life like before."

"That won't happen. I promise."

"What will happen?"

"With us?" When she nodded, he went on. "I think it's too soon to be going there."

"You're probably right."

"There's no probably about it."

"Bossy, aren't you?"

"I am the king."

She wiggled against him. "Then why are you on the bottom?"

HE FLIPPED HER over. She tickled him, this Milla, getting back the spark she'd been missing. "Who's your daddy, now?"

"Finally. I was wondering if I was going to have to stay up there forever."

A memory flared up. "Ah, yes. My little missionary sex fiend."

"It's just…cozy down here." She snuggled deeper into the mattress.

Yeah. Cozy was exactly what he was going for. "Cozy?"

"I like feeling your weight, and rubbing my feet over your calves. When I'm on top, it's all about the peg and the hole."

"As it should be."

She rolled her eyes. "Men."

"When you're riding me like a cowgirl, I don't have a head for anything else."

"Then it's true. Sex is all about the small head? Rather than the big one?"

He glared down at her. "Who're you calling small?"

She slapped him on the shoulder. "You know what I mean."

This time he made sure he had her attention. And that she knew this wasn't a game. "When I think about making love to you, it's not just about the big guy downstairs. But when he's doing his thing? Yeah. There's not a lot of activity going on above the belt."

She considered him for a moment, circling his nipples with her thumbs. "I guess I can live with that. As long as I know you do think about more than getting me naked."

"I never said that."

"I'm going to have to hurt you now."

"I survived you breaking my heart," he said without thinking, hoping to distract her by adding, "What's a bone or two between friends?"

She grew still. And silent. Her eyes filled with tears. "Did I really break your heart?"

"I let you," he said, his voice gruff.

"That doesn't make me feel any better."

"Does this make you feel better?"

She nodded.

"What about this?"

"God, yes."

"Then nothing else really matters."

SHE BUCKED UPWARD and knocked him over. Correction. He let her knock him over. This was a strange exchange of power, and she wasn't quite sure what to do with it.

She glared down. "I want to talk about your heart."

"Fine," he said, grabbing one of her hands and settling it on his chest. "It's here. It's beating. What else is there to say?"

"There's so much to say. I don't even know where to start."

"We did a dumb thing, sneaking around. Dating other people to cover our tracks."

"No kidding."

"But I was a grease monkey and you were a society girl. I get why it happened."

She shook her head. "That's not why it happened."

"Sure it is. You were doing what was expected of you with Derek and doing what you wanted to do with me. I should've hiked up my pride and put a stop to it, but I was too crazy in love—"

"Stop saying that." She slapped at his chest, so frustrated, so...hurt.

He grabbed her hand. "You want to go back to lying? I thought we agreed to tell the whole truth and nothing but."

She hung her head. "We did."

"Is this where I pull a Jack Nicholson then? Tell you you can't handle the truth?"

Tears spilled, and she couldn't stop them. She could barely find her voice. "I never let myself believe that you loved me. That we were together for anything more than the sex. I'd convinced myself that I wasn't your type—"

"What kind of crap is that?" he snapped.

"Let me finish. Looking at the girls you dated? I wasn't. I'm not busty and leggy. I was never a party girl. I was your tutor. The girl with her head in the books."

"I dated them because I couldn't have you," he said so honestly she jumped.

"You never told me you wanted me."

"GODDAMN, MILLA," he said, switching their positions again and glaring down. "I told you that every time I sunk my body into yours."

"That was sex. We talked about it. We agreed. There couldn't be anything between us but sex."

"Then you kept up your end of the bargain a lot better than I did."

"But I didn't. I didn't keep it up at all. I fell in love with you. How could I not. You made me laugh. You made me think. You taught me how to change my own oil," she said, her laughter catching on a sobbing intake of breath. "I loved you, Rennie. You gave me all the things Derek didn't have it in him to give."

"But you stayed with him anyway," he said, his chest aching, his throat on fire. Damn her. Just damn her. And damn him, as well.

"I didn't know you wanted more."

"I did. But I don't think either one of us was ready for that. Not then." He wasn't even sure they were ready now.

Or if it was even smart to consider trying.

12

Seven years ago…

MILLA SAT in the university library, her laptop humming, Shakespearean texts fanned out around her, her backpack in the chair to her left. She'd chosen the table farthest from the librarian's counter and the constant flow of traffic in and out of the front door.

Rennie was late, and she was doing her best not to get mad. She'd agreed to help him with his term paper. That did not mean it was her job to act as his keeper. If he wasn't interested, fine. He could fail. She wasn't going to waste her own valuable study time waiting.

And she certainly wasn't going to start wondering who he was with. She was his tutor. That was all. The fact that they stole time to sleep together whenever they could did not mean they were in a relationship. He didn't owe her anything.

And she didn't need to be wondering how he was spending his time. That was totally unproductive and a ridiculous distraction when her own grades were in serious need of her time and attention.

She turned back to the paragraph she'd left unfinished, trying to analyze both the Montagues and the Capulets while keeping the complicated dynamics of the Page and Randall families from coloring her thoughts.

She didn't like the hints her parents were dropping about her future with Derek. They'd even teased her about grandchildren when she wasn't close to being ready for a commitment of that sort. Not yet—no matter how much her parents were counting on her making the match they'd deemed beneficial.

Thinking about her life and her personal relationships was a distraction as disturbing as thinking about Rennie—especially since it was getting harder to separate the first from the second.

It didn't matter how many times she reminded herself that Rennie was an infatuation. He was the one she saw in her future, the future she wanted, not the future of her parents' matchmaking.

God, she should never have kissed Rennie that first time in the dorm. She should never have volunteered to tutor him. She should never have gotten carried away with him at the Incubus concert, thinking they had a chance at…something.

She slumped back in her chair and closed her eyes. When had she turned into such a drama queen, fretting about what couldn't be changed instead of focusing on what could? What was done, was done. She could only move forward, make better decisions, be the one in charge of her life from now on—not the one who let everyone else mow her down.

Looking up, she reached for her legal pad of notes but got no further. Rennie was walking down the center aisle between the tables toward her, and her heart skipped a half a dozen beats.

He was wearing the same thing he always wore, blue jeans, a white T-shirt and black biker boots. She couldn't imagine him in anything else. Neither could she count the heads that turned in his wake.

It was so unfair that he had that effect on people. He took over a room, intimidating those around him—the same ones who cut him down to make themselves look better. She'd seen it happen, hated when it did, wanted to jump to Rennie's defense but never found the courage.

Still, she couldn't help but thrill at the tingle that tickled her toes when she thought about him being on his way to see her. Infatuation wasn't even the half of it. She had fallen for him completely, and didn't know what she was going to do.

"Sorry I'm late," he said, slipping into the chair on her right. "I got caught up at work."

"Why were you at work in the middle of the day?" He smelled so good. He'd just showered, and his clothes were clean, and she wanted to bury her face in his skin and just breathe. "Didn't you have class this morning?"

He nodded. "We were in the middle of an engine rebuild and needed it finished today."

"So you skipped class for work?"

He slouched back in the chair, cut his gaze toward her, shook back his hair. "I've been at work since yesterday. We worked all night and still aren't done. I only left so I could meet up with you."

Focus. She had to focus. She couldn't think of anything but school. She clenched her hands tightly in her lap. "Good. I was starting to wonder if you cared at all about your grades."

"I care about the degree. About Shakespeare?" He shook his head, his hair curling over his T-shirt's band. "Not so much. I can't see how the bard's going to do me any good in a garage."

"What if you do something else with your life? Other than work on cars?"

"It's a family business, Milla. It's pretty much set in stone."

"So, you're doing it because it's what's expected?" If so, would he understand that she was doing what she had to do, too?

"No. I'm doing it because it's what I love."

She knew that, but still she asked, "You've never thought about doing anything else?"

"Why? Would something else make me more respectable?" He leaned in closer. "If I switch gears and do the med school thing, can we stop sneaking around?"

She took a deep breath, stared at her hands. "We have to stop sneaking around, but your career path has nothing to do with it."

Rennie took a minute to respond, and she closed her eyes when she felt him stiffen, sensing the moment he scooted forward into her space by the heat that came with him. Why did this have to be so hard?

"I don't get what you're saying, Milla. You want to go public? To be a couple for real?" When she didn't respond right away, he moved even closer. Her hair feathered against her neck, blown there as he whispered, "That's not it at all, is it? You're breaking things off."

Funny, but doing that had not been her intention when she'd sat down to wait for him, but suddenly she knew it was the right thing to do.

She didn't want to keep living a lie. And she didn't want to fall any harder for Rennie and worsen the inevitable hurt. "We're not being fair to anyone—"

"Damn it, Milla," Rennie barked, causing heads to turn and Milla to open her eyes and shush him. He lowered his voice. "Would you think of yourself for once? What you want? What makes you happy?"

"Being selfish isn't making me happy, Rennie."

"You seemed happy enough skipping Derek's game yesterday afternoon."

She'd promised her boyfriend she'd be there for the charity football game he was quarterbacking. She'd spent the time in bed with Rennie instead. "At the time, I was. But today I can't stop thinking about how many people we're hurting."

"We're not hurting anyone. No one knows."

"That doesn't make it right. It's still a lie."

"And breaking things off won't change that."

"It won't change what we've done, no. But at least the lie will go away."

"Right. You'll just be lying to yourself instead. Telling yourself you and Derek were meant for each other. Telling him that you love him—"

"I do love him—"

"Telling yourself that being with me is about nothing but sex—"

"It is only sex—"

"One lie on top of another, Milla. You're doing it even now."

He was right. She knew in her heart that everything he said was true. She lifted her hands, her fingers hovering over the laptop, the words on the screen blurring as she stared.

"I don't know what to do," she whispered softly. "It's too hard—"

"It's not hard," he said with a desperate growl. "It's not. You do what you want to do."

What she wanted to do would hurt too many people. Her parents, the Randalls…Derek. But doing what she felt she had to do would hurt the one person it would kill her to wrong.

Maybe she didn't have to do it all at once. Maybe she could figure something out if she gave herself time. "Can we just take a break? For a little while? I just need…space. To decide what to do."

"If you want to dump me, there's nothing to decide." He shifted around in his chair, slamming it up against the table. "Say the words. I'm gone."

That wasn't what she wanted, but she didn't know if it was possible for them to go to back to the beginning. Or if they could be simply friends. "I don't want you to go anywhere. All I'm asking for is time to get my head together."

She turned toward him then, her eyes still watery, which was probably a good thing. His eyes were dark brown and no clearer than hers. God, she hated making him sad. "Can you give me that at least?"

"How long?"

"I don't know." She rubbed at her forehead. "A few days. A couple of weeks, maybe."

Rennie sorted. "You sure you don't want to make it months and years?"

She didn't want to make it anything at all. She wanted to grab Rennie by the hand, leave school and never look back. She wanted to travel the country and enjoy being alive instead of feeling trapped.

She ran the heels of her palms beneath her eyes and sniffed loudly enough that several heads turned. "Let's just work on the outline for your paper, okay?"

"Whatever," he grumbled, but having him grumble was better than having him so angry and hurt that he walked out of her life for good.

"IT'S BOOTY CALL TIME," Amy said, scurrying away from Milla's office door before she had a chance to look up from her screen.

When she did, it was to find Natalie standing there. "Booty call time for some of us. For Amy, it's a nature call."

Milla smiled, looked back at her laptop screen. "I'm not going."

"Why not?" Natalie asked, walking into the room, her skirt swinging as she settled into the visitor's chair with a flourish. "Still wondering which of the sisters had her hands on your man."

"This isn't about who had their hands on Rennie. And he's not my man." *Liar, liar, pants on fire.* "I'm busy. I've got to get my review of Minstrel's Merlot written up. Then see if I can get next weekend's review of High Notes assigned to someone else."

"You know Joan's not going to let that happen," Natalie said. "You're the site's reviewer. You're the single one of the bunch. You're the expert on what makes a place worth recommending."

"Whatever," Milla said.

"Girl, have you not seen the e-mail that's come in since the profile of Test Flight was posted? People are loving the place. It's generated a lot of buzz and some new business."

She had seen it, and it was satisfying in a job-well-done sort of way. That didn't change the fact that she wanted nothing more than to stay in with a good book and a tub of chocolate-chip ice cream. "I just don't feel like spending another Friday night at a club."

Natalie pursed her lips and frowned. "And none of this is about the man who's not your man."

"Nope." Milla shook her head emphatically, trying to convince the both of them. "I just thought it would be nice to give someone else the shot at a byline."

"You are so full of it I have to wonder what you've been eating at these restaurants."

So much for being convincing, Milla mused. "I have no idea. I can barely remember what the service was like. Or the decor. Except for the eggplant."

"What eggplant?"

"Nothing. Never mind. Ignore me."

"I will," Natalie said, getting out of the chair and heading to the door, closing it just as she'd done last week. "Now. Forget the sisters and the booty and the review. I want to know what is going on with you and Rennie. Besides all the sex."

"Who said we're having sex?"

"The glow on your face and your bow-legged gait. Spill. I want details."

Milla abandoned the review and slumped back in her chair. "He told me that he used to be crazy in love with me."

"Used to be."

"Yep."

"Back when you were having wild and secret college sex."

"Yep."

"What about now?"

"Now we're having wild and not-so-secret but casually convenient post-college sex."

"And the love part?" Natalie asked.

Milla shook her head. "I don't know."

"Don't know if he still loves you? Or if you still love him?"

"He hasn't told me anything. And I'm afraid to tell him how I feel."

"Why are you afraid?"

Could it be any more obvious? "Because that means I have to admit it to myself."

"Uh, girlfriend? You just did," Natalie said, and Milla took a moment to see how the reality fit…

Not so well. "God, Natalie. What am I going to do?" She crossed her forearms on her desk and collapsed against them. "I can't be in love with him. I can't."

"Why not? Because he sells cars for a living?"

"He restores cars." She sat back up. "He doesn't sell them. And, no. That has nothing to do with it. He has money. And that doesn't have anything to do with it, either."

"Are you two talking about your past relationship?"

"We're circling a lot of it, but yeah. We're talking."

"And you're getting somewhere with all that talk?"

Milla shrugged. "I don't know. We've only been out the two times."

"That's it? Those are the only times you've seen him?"

"Yep."

"How much of that time was spent in bed?"

"A lot."

"And you want me to believe that you managed to stick some quality talking time in there?"

"He called me one night last week. We talked then."

"Whoop-diddly-do." Natalie tapped her fingernails on the chair arm. "You and your man need to spend time together out of bed. You know you're compatible between the sheets. And that's important. Don't get me wrong. I *know* that's important."

Natalie leaned forward. "But there is a lot of stuff that matters more. And that's the stuff you have to be sure of, because sex isn't big enough by itself to hold things together."

"I know that." God, did she ever. "But sometimes I think sex is all Rennie and I have."

"Then cut him off."

"What? Why?"

"Never mind cutting him off. Cut yourself off. Take a celibacy vow. It's all the rage, you know. The two of you need time."

"We've had six years."

"No, you haven't. You may have been thinking about him that long, but not one day during those six years have the two of you done so much as laid eyes on each other. All you've done is pout."

"Have not."

"Pouted just like you're pouting now."

"I'm only pouting because I skipped breakfast and it's too early for lunch."

"Who says?"

"Joan would if she were here," Milla said, desperate to find a way out of doing the right thing.

"She's not, so go. Take a long one. Find someone tall, dark and sexy to go with you." Natalie leaned forward and pointed her finger at Milla. "And don't come back until the two of you have talked."

13

"WHAT WAS THAT all about," Rennie asked, watching Hector watching Angie as she flounced out of the garage office. "She on your case about the filing again?"

"Not about the filing," Hector said, heading back inside. "About the art."

"Art?" Rennie asked, following.

Hector turned, gestured with one hand. "I was stupid enough to tell her that I'd never decorated my place. She took me shopping on Saturday. For art."

Rennie tried not to laugh, but the humor got the better of him. "And? How's her taste, because I know you don't have any."

"I don't. Which is the very reason my walls have nothing on them but paint."

"Hey, you could've had an autographed 'Hell on Wheels' poster if you'd asked."

Hector rolled his eyes, wiped a red shop rag over his head. "I'm working on separating my work life from my personal life, but thanks."

"Things with you and Angie are going well, then?"

"We shopped for art. Not wedding bands."

"What did you get?"

"Some real nice pictures done by some National Geographic photographer. It's a series taken in Central America. Some animals, a coffee plantation, mountains. Stuff like that. Lots of green. She figured they'd go best with the white walls and brown leather couch."

"That'll work. Of course I still think a 'Hell on Wheels' poster would be the thing."

Hector flipped Rennie a finger. "You can take your damn poster and shove it—"

"Excuse me."

At the sound of Milla's voice, Rennie spun around. "Hey, you. What are you doing here?"

She stepped hesitantly into the office. "I'm sorry to interrupt—"

"You're not. I was just giving Hector here a hard time, and I'm sure he'll be more than glad for me to go away."

Hector walked out from around the desk and offered Milla his hand. "Hector Prieto."

She accepted it and smiled. "Milla Page."

"You a fan of Rennie's?" Hector asked

Rennie hurried to cut him off. He wasn't ready to tell Milla about the show. "Milla and I went to USF together. She was my tutor, and I roomed with an ex of hers for a year."

"I thought maybe she was here about you needing some art," Hector said on his way out, slapping Rennie on the shoulder and adding, "It's nice to meet you, Milla."

"You, too," she said, waiting until after Hector was gone to ask, "What was that about art?"

"Nothing," Rennie said, desperate to change the subject and to get Milla out of the garage. He'd tell her about "Hell on Wheels" eventually. Just not today.

"What brings you by?" he asked, surprised how glad he was to see her.

"A couple of things, really."

"I've got an office in the showroom. Let's talk there where there's less chance of you getting something foul on your clothes." He placed a palm in the small of her back, guiding her in that direction. "You look great, by the way."

"You mean, I look colorful?" she asked, a tinge of self-deprecation in her voice.

She did, but he couldn't say if it was the purple and orange in her dress responsible for the blush of her skin, or if it was just Milla coming back to life. "You can wear any color and look great. I don't know why you'd settle for black."

"Because it goes with everything and is easy to accessorize," she said as they stepped out into the late-autumn sun and through the showroom's back door.

They were halfway down the narrow hallway to his office when he careened to a stop. He'd been giving Hector a hard time about "Hell on Wheels" posters when he had three of them framed and hanging on his own office walls. *Son of a barking dog.*

"What's wrong?" Milla asked, turning when she realized he was no longer beside her.

"I'm starving," he blurted. "Let's grab some something to eat."

She glanced at her watch, her lips bowing.

"Do you have time?"

"Actually, I do. Natalie, one of my coworkers, shoved me out the door and told me she'd cover for me while I took a long lunch."

"She thought you needed one?" he asked, taking her elbow and leading her back out the door to the lot where he parked the truck he drove during the week.

Milla laughed softly, hiking up her skirt and stepping onto the running board to climb into the passenger seat. She waited until he'd circled the truck and settled behind the wheel before going on. "I spent all morning working on my review and got nowhere. She suggested I take a break."

"You guys watch out for each other then," he said, putting the truck into reverse, his arm along the back of the seat brushing her shoulder.

She nodded. "Amy and Natalie are great friends. Amy's married and very pregnant, and Natalie's engaged. Her fiancé is a surgical resident at St. Luke's, and has been my source of men for a while."

He glanced over. "I thought you drew business cards from the boot."

"At times. But since my dates are mostly working dates, it's easier to go out with a friend who knows the score."

"Instead of a guy who wants to get you naked, you mean," he said, happier than made sense to hear the truth.

"Yeah," she said, laughing softly. "Though that's

usually not much of a concern when they realize I mean it when I say a date is strictly business."

"What about dates that aren't business?" Her personal life, the lovers she'd had since they'd split...none of that was need-to-know. But it didn't stop him from asking.

She held her purse clutched in her lap. "I can't remember the last one I had. Like I said before, working for a dating service has put me off the whole relationship game."

Interesting. "If you think about it as a game, no wonder."

"Isn't that what it is?" she asked, with no small amount of sarcasm. "How many points do you have to score with your partner to win?"

He frowned and glanced over. She was looking straight ahead as they drove. "Is that really how you look at relationships?"

She took a few moments to answer, her tone wistful when she finally did. "When I see what Amy and Natalie have, no. But when I hear stories from clients who've gone through two dozen possible candidates, well, it's hard to know what to think."

"Not everyone gets it right the first time out," he said, thinking of their past.

"Or the first twenty-plus times?"

"It can happen. Don't let the repeat offenders sour you on relationships."

"I think I was soured before I ever went to work at MatchMeUp. That whole atmosphere was just the final straw."

Rennie took the turn into the lot of a neighborhood restaurant, a small family place that served the best enchiladas he'd ever eaten. He parked the truck, but he left the engine running.

He didn't like thinking that he had been the first straw, that as badly as his own heart had been damaged, that he'd been responsible for Milla breaking apart. "If I did that to you, I'm sorry. It was never intentional, hurting you."

"I don't know if you did it or not. It could have been what you and I did to Derek. It could have been my parents' expectations. Or even the way they treated each other."

She took a deep breath, dropped her head against the back of the seat. "It was probably a combination of all of it. And, no. It didn't help that the only time I've ever been in love, the relationship was a lie."

He couldn't think of anything to say. She'd just told him she'd once loved him. It was the first time she'd ever used the word. He wanted to know why she'd waited so long, why she'd waited until it was too late, but then he realized he'd done the very same thing.

He'd loved her. He'd never told her. He'd been so wrapped up in being with her, in not losing what they had, that he never thought beyond seizing the freakin' day. And now they were both paying for those things they'd done wrong.

"Hey, Mr. Mechanic. Are you going to feed me? Or are we just going to sit here all day feeling sorry for ourselves?"

At Milla's question, he looked over, surprised to

see her eyes sparkling when the mood in the truck—
at least on the driver's side—had turned so dark.

"You never did tell me why you dropped by," he
noted, pushing open his door and climbing down.

Milla answered once he'd reached her side. "It's
about Friday. The club we're going to. It's fairly
upscale. I just wanted you to know."

"You could have called to tell me that."

"I know," she said, and those two words answered
every question he could have asked.

"What's the name of the club?"

"High Notes."

Uh-oh. The owner was a major "Hell on Wheels"
fan and a golf buddy of Rennie's. He'd have to make
a call, forewarning and forearming and all that. "I'll
pick you up at eight?"

"Perfect."

"Okay, then. Let's knock back some enchiladas."

HECTOR HAD JUST STEPPED out of the shower on
Thursday night when he heard a knock on the door. He
dropped his towel to the bedroom floor, grabbed his
boxers and sweats and yanked them on, then headed
out into the living room.

Since he wasn't expecting anyone, he checked
through the peephole to see if he even wanted to answer. His visitor brought a smile to his face, and a
feeling of anticipation socked him in the gut.

"Is this a habit of yours?" he asked, opening the
door. "Showing up when a guy's not expecting you?"

Angie's gaze remained locked with his. She seemed nervous with him being only half dressed while she was still wearing the tropical print skirt and blouse she'd worn to work today. "I wanted to see how the photographs looked. I figured I stood a better chance of getting through your door if I didn't give you any warning."

Typical Angie Soon. Saying what was on her mind. Expecting to get her way. None of it selfish or malicious. It was just who she was.

"Come in, then. I'll get a shirt. The photographs are on the wall above the couch."

He shut the door behind her and returned to his bedroom, grabbing a gray athletic T-shirt from the closet where he hung everything since he'd never bothered with a chest of drawers.

When he got back to the living room, Angie was standing on the far side of the coffee table facing the couch. "Since I hadn't seen how your place was laid out, I wasn't sure how these would look."

He walked over to stand beside her, waiting for her to say more, but she didn't. She had one arm crossed over her middle, her fingers wrapped around the strap of her shoulder bag, the elbow of her other arm braced on top, her index finger tapping the top of her lip.

"Well?" he finally prodded when it seemed as if she wasn't going to share her opinion after all. "Are you good with the walls?"

"Yes," she said, circling the table to get a closer look. "The lamps make all the difference."

She'd made him buy a pair, one for each end of the

couch. Both had three separate arms with different watt bulbs. He'd snaked them this way and that, turned on some switches, turned others off, realizing while experimenting that Angie knew what she was talking about.

The entire living area looked much more…alive. It pulsed and breathed with all the things he'd known growing up, all the things he'd experienced, and he couldn't help but miss his family and home.

"The lamps are great," he finally said, inhaling a steadying breath and adding, "Thank you. It is more comfortable here now. I didn't think decorating would make a difference."

He saw her smile in profile. "Not all decorating has to go as overboard as my mamma's. You can get a nice look with only a little extra effort. It just has to be the right effort."

She was still facing away from him, and he wondered what it was she was searching for in the photographs. Or if she was only admiring her handiwork. The simple look she'd put together for him was so much different than what he'd seen at her home.

He wondered if it was only taking care of her mother that was keeping her there, or if it was something else she hadn't told him. Some reason she couldn't get her own place and do her care-taking from there.

"You have a good eye," he finally said because Angie's life wasn't his concern. "I'll bet you'll do a great job fixing up your own digs when you move out of your mamma's place."

After a long quiet minute, Angie sighed and turned

to sit on his couch. She held her purse in her lap and sat just on the cushion's edge, staring at her hands where her fingers were laced, looking strangely nervous and unsure. "I don't know, Hector. If I can live on my own."

He frowned, uneasy, not sure what was the best thing for him to say. "You can't afford it? What with supporting your mother, too?"

She shook her head. "It's not money. Bergen's pays me enough. More than my last job did."

He started to ask what it was, then stopped because her voice seemed shaky and she was holding her hands together so tightly it looked as if her skin would split. "You want a soda or something? I've got Dr Pepper. And Orange Crush."

"Sure. But I can get it," she said, rising to her feet.

"It's my house, Angie," he said over his shoulder as she followed him into the kitchen. "I'm supposed to be the one waiting on you."

She tried to laugh, but it sounded more like a chirp. "I'm just so used to doing everything for everyone. It's hard to let anyone do anything for me."

An alarm went off in his head as he reached into the fridge for two bottles. He pried off the tops then opened a cabinet. "All I've got is a mug, is that okay?"

"I can drink from the bottle," she said. "But, Hector. Why don't you have more than mugs?" She pulled open a second cabinet next to the first. Then she pulled open a third before she turned. "Hector. There's nothing here."

"There's enough," he said, sipping his drink, wondering where her concern came from, what it meant. "I don't need more."

"But do you really not want more? Are you the one who needs to ask Rennie for a raise?"

Hector laughed, walked back into the living room and sat on one end of the couch. Angie sat on the edge of the other, placing her purse and her soda on his coffee table.

"Tell me something, Hector," she said, glancing over, her knees pressed firmly together, her bare lips momentarily pressed into a straight line. "Now, this isn't any of my business, so don't think I expect you to answer, but what do you do with all of your money?"

He cocked back in the corner of the couch, draped one arm along the back, the other holding his bottle along the tufted arm. "Remember me telling you about my village."

"Hector, I am trying to be serious here. I am worried that you are maybe into something you shouldn't be."

He watched her gaze drift to the tattoo on his neck before she cut it sharply away. It was as though she wanted to know his history, but she didn't want to ask or to risk making accusations.

He wondered if something about the tattoo frightened her, if she knew what it was. "I'm not gambling or into drugs, if that's what you're asking."

"I didn't really think that you were," she said, though she didn't sound completely convinced. "But we work together, and I care about you, so I had to ask."

He took his time shifting to sit forward, bracing his elbows on his knees and holding his bottle between both hands. "I've done some things that ain't so nice, Angie. In the past. You probably need to know that. I was only sixteen when I got here, and I was on my own, so I made some decisions that weren't the best."

"What sort of decisions?" she asked softly, reaching for her drink as if she needed something to hold.

He'd put the subject on the table. He could hardly take it back now. It just wasn't so easy to talk about with her sitting so close and smelling so gentle and sweet. "Like I said. I came here by myself. I didn't know any-one, and I hooked up with some guys who turned out to be pretty bad, even though they were really good to me."

"Gang-bangers?"

He nodded. "I was pretty dumb way back then. Fresh off the boat, or whatever the saying is."

"But, Hector." She started to reach out but pulled back her hand. "Why would you come here all alone? Did you not know anyone at all?"

He thought back to the trip he'd made all the way through Guatemala and Mexico to the border, and he wished Angie wasn't afraid to touch him. He wanted very much to hold on to her hand. "My parents raised the money to pay a *coyote* to get me into the States. I was supposed to hook up with a cousin who worked on a farm. I ended up in L.A. instead."

Angie curled her legs beneath her and settled deeper

into the corner of the couch. She smoothed her skirt over her knees, staring at the fabric when she spoke. "So when you told me about your village, you were serious."

He'd known when he'd first mentioned his village that she'd thought he was being a smart-ass. He'd let it go because it wasn't so important what she thought of him when he was fine with himself.

But now that it seemed they were getting closer and more familiar, that she really did want to know more about who he was and who he'd been, now what she thought of him was more important, and she needed to know the truth.

He wasn't a good catch. Period. He had too many other people relying on him. Family who wouldn't have a thing if he didn't provide it, leaving him little for himself, and nothing to offer a woman. And that didn't even take into consideration his crimes.

"No. I was serious," he told her. "My parents and grandparents live there with my uncles and aunts and cousins and my four sisters. I send them everything I make except what I need to live on."

"Don't you mean, survive on?"

"No, because I could survive on less."

"Why would you?"

"So that they could have more," he said, and got to his feet, wishing for once that he did have a bigger place so he had somewhere besides his bedroom to go to, to get away from Angie's questions.

Instead he turned to study the photographs she'd

brought into his home, realizing as he studied them that it was his own guilt he was wanting to escape.

It wasn't right that he still had so much when his family would never have everything they needed—or the one thing they wanted most of all.

"How long has it been since you've seen them?" Angie asked as if she'd been reading his mind.

"I haven't been back since I left," he said, and she gasped, but he went on before she could speak. "At first it wasn't smart, being illegal and all. I wasn't sure I'd ever get back if I left."

"But you're legal now, right?"

He nodded. "I was eighteen when I came up here. I spoke English and had references from a couple of places I'd worked in L.A. Bergen hired me on to do odd jobs and all, and then Rennie's dad called in some favors and helped me get legal."

"You still never went back to see your family?"

"I decided it was more important to be able to support them. That's why they'd sent me here. I didn't want to let them down."

He fell silent then, and Angie did, too, but he felt her as she came to stand beside him. She was small, but her presence was large, and she warmed him there where she stood at his side.

"What do you see in the photographs, Hector? What do you think about when you look at them?"

More things than he would ever be able to tell her. "My cousin Ramon. We used to do a lot of fishing in a lake a couple of miles from where we lived. We'd build fires and stay for days and talk about coming to the States. We thought that if we could do that, we'd never have anything to worry about again."

Angie slipped her arm through his. "Did Ramon come over when you did?"

Hector shook his head, his throat closing up. "He came a few months before. Or he was supposed to anyway."

"He didn't make it?" she asked, squeezing his arm, her fingers strong, her voice no more than a whisper.

"No one knows. It's been twelve years. We haven't heard from him." Hector cleared his throat. "My family thinks that the connections I have here mean I should be able to find out what happened."

"Is that why you don't go home? Why you send all your money there? Because you don't have any answers and don't want to face them?"

How did she know? How could she? He'd never told anyone about Ramon. Not the street family he'd run with during his years in L.A. Not any of his coworkers since, or the Bergens.

He'd kept it bottled up all this time, thinking it was his problem, that no one else would understand. That no one else would ever get the guilt he felt at failing his family in a way all his money would never make right.

But Angie… He took a deep breath. "Yeah. That's pretty much it."

This time she didn't ask him any more questions or say anything at all. All she did was lean close and lay her head on his shoulder, squeeze his arm where she held it, and rub his chest with her other hand.

He let her. He didn't even wonder what she was thinking. He stood there and let her soothe him, let her share in the burden he carried.

And for the first time in many many years, he didn't feel alone.

14

"Wow. Just wow," Milla said on Friday night after she and Rennie had been shown to one of High Notes' small tables that were scattered in and out of the room's screens and floral arrangements.

"What?" he asked, frowning as he smiled.

"Last week you looked amazing. But tonight…" She drank him in, shaking her head. "Is it too much of a cliché to say you look good enough to eat?"

"Not if you mean it," he leaned close to say. When she stuck out her tongue playfully in answer, he laughed and added, "I do know how to dress, Milla. I told you that before."

"I know," she said, settling into her chair, placing her purse on the table. "It's just part of the job, making sure everything runs smoothly on the assignments. I forget most people don't need the reminder."

"How's the job going? Are the advertisers happy?"

She nodded. "So far, so good. I mean, it's only been a couple of weeks, but our office has had a ton of new clients take the plunge."

"You write good reviews."

She shrugged. "I'm not sure it's that as much as seeing our stats compared to those from around the country. People like to be a part of putting their city on top."

He glanced around what he could see of the room as they settled into their seats. "So what's the draw of this place?"

"It's classy without being pretentious," she said, following the direction of his gaze. "And it's quiet. The perfect place to have a private conversation without having to worry about being overheard." She looked back at him then and smiled. "It's a good place to enjoy good company, to be comfortable, to steal a few kisses."

He waggled both brows. "All the more reason to dress for the occasion, right?"

She sighed. "You know, coming to see you on Monday was totally spur of the moment, and dressing for tonight was the only reason I could come up with for the visit."

"It showed." He couldn't help it. He had to give her a hard time for going back on her honesty vow. "Lies have a way of coming back to bite you."

"Sorry," she said, toying with the gold clasp on her purse. "But the truth was just too lame to admit."

"What was the truth?" he asked a few minutes later after giving the server his order of a Scotch on the rocks and hers of a mango margarita.

"I don't know. I mean, I don't know why I came. Except to see you." She dropped her gaze to her lap where her fingers were tangled up in the ends of the sash she wore tied low on her hips. "I just wanted to see you."

He took a minute to let what she'd told him sink in. She was opening up, and he didn't want to say anything to stop it. "It's okay, you know. You don't have to have any other reason. In fact, I like that you wanted to see me. I like it a lot."

"It just seems so… I don't know." She laced her hands together, returned them to the edge of the table, stared down at her fingers as she spoke. "I can't figure out what we're doing, Rennie. Or where we're going."

He didn't like her questioning what felt so right. He wanted her to enjoy their shared desire to move beyond the past, not analyze the ins and outs. "Is it something we have to figure out? Right now? Tonight?"

"Not tonight, no. Eventually?" She nodded. "Yes. And I know there's no timetable on eventually, but I just feel…"

"Feel what, Milla?" he asked, growing frustrated as their server arrived with their drinks.

Once the other woman was gone, Milla threaded her fingers around the stem of her glass. "I feel as if we've wasted so much time. We've hurt each other. We've hurt so many other people."

"And we're working through all of that."

"But what if we can't get beyond it? What if we still can't get what we want, and all of this has been an exercise in trying to salvage a lost cause?"

Strangely enough, what she said gave him hope when on the surface it should have strangled him. The fact that she was worried meant he wasn't the only one here emotionally involved. "What do you want?"

"I'm not sure I even know," she murmured, lifting her drink, but her denial rang false.

He was certain that she did know. He was also certain she felt that putting it out there would be jeopardizing their uneasy truce. He pushed anyway. He had to because she was right. They'd wasted too much time already, and tonight was the last night they were guaranteed to have this quiet and private time.

"Do you want to keep seeing me? After tonight? Seeing *me*," he continued, cutting her off before she could answer only part of the question. "Seeing me because you want to be with me, not because I'm a convenient date when you need one for work?"

The lights in the room lowered and the club's pianist took the stage. A soft jazzy melody floated down around them and Rennie reached over to take hold of Milla's hands.

She looked up, tears shimmering in her bright-green eyes. "I want that more than anything, but I'm so incredibly frightened."

"Don't be. We don't have to do this now. Let's just listen to the music," he said, his voice growing husky, his body growing tense, his patience unfortunately in very short supply. If he screwed this up, he was a dead man. He'd see to it himself.

He shifted his chair around so that he could drape his arm over the back of hers, and he pulled her into the curve of his body. She fit against him in a way that no other woman had ever done.

He toyed with the blunt ends of her hair that brushed

her neck and collarbone, stroked his fingertips from shoulder to shoulder where her chest was bared by the low-cut scoop of her dress.

She shivered, her skin pebbling. He thought about how tight her nipples grew when he sucked them into his mouth, how close she came to coming apart when he did, and grew tight himself in response.

"Are you okay?" she turned to whisper at hearing the guttural groan he'd been unable to stop.

He leaned his head closer to hers, continued to tease her, to play her, nibbling on the shell of her ear, nipping at the lobe, tonguing the tiny diamond she wore there. "I'd be a whole lot better if you were straddling me naked."

"Pervert." She dug her shoulder into his chest, her hair tickling his jaw when she moved. "I thought you wanted to listen to the music."

"No, I wanted *you* to listen to the music while I figured a way to get you out of your clothes," he said, and she shuddered as he ran his knuckles along her cleavage. "Seemed it would be easier that way than if we were talking."

She lifted her chin and moaned when he nuzzled the line of her jaw. "Rennie, we can't have a relationship if we don't talk."

Her words caused his heart to thud and his blood to run hot. He nudged his nose to her neck and breathed her in. He wished he was better at separating his emotions from his lust because—right now?—he wasn't sure what he was feeling.

"Do we have a relationship, Milla?" he asked, his

voice hoarse, his throat constricted. He was so damn close to having it all that he ached. "Is that what you want?"

She bowed her head and pulled away, the move nearly ripping him apart. "What I want doesn't matter, Rennie. Not if you can't forgive me."

"For what?" he asked before he could stop himself, then wished for the chance to back up and bite his tongue. He knew what she was going to say, that she was going to that place they hadn't yet been.

She turned then, and faced him, reaching up to cup his cheek, her eyes so bright and open, so filled with raw emotion, and so very close that he had no chance to run and hide. "For what I said in front of everyone at the party. For being that cruel when I loved you so much…"

Six years ago…

"CAN YOU BELIEVE IT?" Milla raised her bottle of beer overhead and twirled around, the stars above twinkling as if it were part of the planned celebration. "We survived all four years without giving up or slitting our wrists!"

Stephanie whooped and hollered. "And we even have a diploma to show for it!"

"Watch out, big, bad world. Here comes big, bad Becca."

"Big, bad and degreed," Risa added while Steph, Becca and Milla all squealed with laughter.

"Oh, my God." Milla was breathless with excitement. "I swear I thought we'd never finish school."

"You're not the only one," Steph said. "I feel like I've been waiting and waiting and wondering if all the agony was worth it."

Risa drank down a quarter of her beer, stepping too close to the edge of the pool before Steph grabbed her back. "All I've got to say is that the suffering had better not be a big waste of time."

"It hasn't been. And it won't be," Becca assured her. "We're all going to be hugely successful. But right now the only thing that matters is that I've got to pee."

"Oh, me, too." Steph hopped from foot to foot. "Where's the bathroom?"

Milla pointed toward the patio door that led into Derek's parents' kitchen. "Through the kitchen to the right. And take Risa with you before she topples into the pool."

"I would never topple," Risa grumbled groggily, more than a little bit drunk. Flanked by Becca and Steph, she continued to complain all the way across the patio. And then she tripped on the step into the kitchen.

Giggling, Milla took a deep breath and dropped into the closest lounge chair, enjoying the music the DJ had chosen to spin and the calm summer night's breeze.

She tuned out the chatter around her, smiled when she heard Derek's laughter from the far end of the pool, and for the first time in ages allowed herself to relax.

With the stress of finals and graduation behind her and her business degree in hand, she was finally in a position to do what she wanted with her life—and with the relationships that had been giving her hell.

First up was explaining to her parents that she was

in no hurry to get married—business merger or not. Whoever she decided to marry was not their call to make.

Derek's parents had already given him the keys to the Randall kingdom, and were even now waiting in Hawaii for him and Milla to join them.

He'd put off the trip for a few days, deciding his first order of business as a college graduate was to throw a party their friends would never forget.

Milla didn't mind the delay. It gave her time to come up with a reason to stay home. If she was ever going to stand on her own, she needed time—and space—to ground herself and find a solid footing.

Time without Derek around, without his parents' good intentions, without her parents' not-so-subtle insistence that she'd make the perfect society wife.

And most of all, time away from the consuming need to be involved with Rennie Bergen.

The break they'd taken from each other last year had only lasted a month. That was it. They'd gone right back to lying, to sneaking around. To getting naked in locations it embarrassed her to think about. It was a wonder she didn't have ulcers with ulcers.

Enough was enough. She had to take charge of her life before she could even consider how anyone else would fit. She didn't want a relationship based on obligation any more than she wanted one based on lies.

The only relationship she wanted was with her business degree and the places it could take her, she mused, pushing up out of the lounger when she caught sight of her girlfriends hurrying back.

"Milla." Steph burst out with her name, having barely caught her breath. "Rennie just got here. He's with Donna Burkhardt."

She knew Rennie dated. He'd never stopped. She also knew the girls he saw were only about passing the time. There was no reason for her to care—or for Steph to think that she would. Unless…

She tightened her grip on her bottle. "And you're telling me this why?"

"Because," Becca said, grabbing Milla's free wrist. "She's drunk off her ass. And I just heard her tell Derek that for the past four years, you've been sleeping with Rennie."

"What?" *Oh. My. God.* She was going to pass out. She swore she was going to pass out. She stumbled backward, Becca's hold the only thing keeping her on her feet. "I don't get it. Why—"

"She was hanging all over Rennie," Risa cut in to say. "I guess she pissed him off. He told her to get lost, and she went straight for Derek."

"God," Milla whispered, panic sweeping through her like a biting wind. "Oh, God."

"It's not true, is it?" Risa asked. "I mean, I know you've tutored him, and you guys have hung out a lot, and he is kinda hot. But would you really screw up what you have with Derek for…a mechanic?"

He's not just a mechanic, she wanted to scream,

hating herself for what she said instead. "Why would you even ask me that? Do you think I'm insane?"

"Leave it to someone like Donna to cause trouble," Becca said with a snort, crossing her arms and glaring across the pool at the commotion. "She doesn't get what she wants so she has to drag someone else down."

"Yeah, don't worry, sweetie," Steph added, wrapping an arm around Milla's shoulders. "We've got your back."

Or they would until they learned the truth, Milla thought in a panic, certain she was about to vomit.

She glanced through the darkness to where Derek was surrounded by the jocks he ran with. She could see them gesturing, pointing, puffing up like roosters about to fight, looking around to see who was on their side.

Her heart began to race, her blood a wildfire burning her up. There were at least a hundred people here tonight, some taking advantage of the Randalls' seven bedrooms, others celebrating privately in the dark corners of the expansive grounds.

But there was still enough of a crowd milling around the pool to make her sweat. Especially since pouncing on gossip was a hobby many here lived for, as was turning a molehill into a mountain of a train wreck.

And then the train wreck headed her way, and what had been a case of nerves became out-and-out dread. Derek was leading the pack, and the pack had surrounded Rennie and was dragging him along.

She wanted to run and hide. She did not want this to happen. Not here. Not now. Not ever. Yeah, she'd known for four years that it could. That didn't mean she was ready. She would never be ready, not for this.

She swallowed hard and lifted her chin, wrapping her arms around her middle and pressing her fists so tight to her body she felt herself bruising her ribs. The pain kept her from feeling anything else, kept fear from settling in.

Derek stopped in front of her, his breath warm with the smell of beer. "I want to know something, Milla," he said without preamble.

It was as if he'd already decided she had to be guilty because it made him look like less of a fool for being so blind. "Are you screwing around with Rennie?"

She'd made the decision to get her life in order. She based her answer on that. "No, and I can't even believe you would ask me such a thing."

"I'm asking because Donna says you've been doing it for four years," Derek said, his eyes bleary but not so much so that it masked his anger.

"Why would you believe anything Donna says?" Milla asked, ignoring the tight knot Donna's friends had formed around the other girl off to the side.

Derek glanced over his shoulder, staring at Rennie for so long that Milla finally looked that way, too. Big mistake. Big, big mistake.

He stood in the center of a circle formed by Derek's friends, older than most of them, taller than several, broader than more than a few. But it wasn't his physicality that set him apart, that drew her gaze, that kept everyone around at a distance.

It was all about his attitude, the look in his eyes, the way he held himself, the explosive sense of danger he carried in every step.

She knew him as well if not better than anyone here, and even she felt the need to stay away—even while at her core she wanted nothing more than to run to him and hold him, to wrap him up in her arms.

Derek stepped directly in front of her then, blocking her gaze and glaring down. "I believe her because Bergen won't deny it. And because you aren't denying it, either."

"There's nothing to deny," she heard herself saying. "Donna doesn't know what she's talking about."

"That's not an answer." Derek loomed above her, fairly growling.

From the corner of her eyes she saw Rennie stiffen. She didn't doubt for a minute that he'd jump in if Derek threatened her. She couldn't let that happen.

She tossed her bottle into the seat of the lounger, shoved her hands to her hips. "What do you want me to say, Derek? You've known me for years, and she gets off on causing trouble. Who are you going to believe?"

"Tell me the truth," he demanded, grabbing hold of her upper arm, jerking her forward. Her girlfriends gasped, and Rennie lunged. Derek's posse manhandled him back into their ring, a pack of wolves having cornered a bear.

She was afraid of what he was going to do. That he would lash out, maul and claw and fight, chew off his own leg and end up hurt, suffering more damage than she could ever inflict with her words.

And so she pushed Derek away, rubbed at the bruise on her arm and asked, "What truth do you want to hear?"

Derek leaned down, his face inches from hers, his fury as palpable as Rennie's. "Are you fucking him?"

"No," she bit off, staring straight into his face as she lied.

"Do you care about him?" His voice grew to a roar. "Do you want to be with him? Is he more to you than an old roommate of mine who you tutor?"

"No," she heard herself saying. "He doesn't mean a thing to me at all. He never has. He never will."

"I FORGAVE YOU a long time ago, Milla," Rennie said, reaching up to dab the moisture that shimmered at the corners of her eyes. "I didn't think I'd ever have the chance to tell you. I didn't know if you'd believe me if I did."

"I want to. God, but I don't know why you're even talking to me." She pulled a tissue from her purse and dried her face, nearly shredding the cloth before she finished. "I treated you so horribly. I'm not even sure if I've forgiven myself."

Forgiving her had been easy once he'd admitted to himself how much he loved her. Too bad he'd been thousands of miles away on the other side of the planet when he'd finally figured it all out.

He pulled the tissue from her hands, tossed it to the table. "You need to. It's over and done with, and we both survived. You've got to let it go."

"I know." She sucked in a huge breath. "And I have. Really."

"Are you sure?"

She nodded, sank back into his body's curve. "I probably wouldn't have been able to if not for seeing you again. I needed to hear you say things were okay."

She smelled so good. So damn good. "Then I guess it worked out that you were hard up for a date."

She laughed softly, the sound as musical as the jazz the pianist played. "I was so envious of you for being able to leave and work things out."

He thought about those weeks and months, about being alone. About how tired he'd been. Working himself. Driving himself. "It wasn't all fun and games, Milla."

"I know. But at the time? I wished that you'd taken me with you."

"I would have if you'd asked," he said, stroking her hair.

"Aren't we the perfect commercial for miscommunication?" Another quiet laugh. "I didn't ask because I thought you never wanted to see me again."

He had to be honest. "For a while, I didn't. I had a lot of growing up to do, and a lot of hurt to get over."

She angled around to better see him. Her bottom lip trembled, her eyes so sad. "I'm so sorry, Rennie. I don't think I can say it enough."

"You have said it enough," he assured her. He'd had plenty of apologies for one night, and told her so with a sharply arched brow.

Her lip stopped trembling and her eyes took on a different sheen. "Are you saying I talk too much?"

He laughed. "You worry too much. You analyze too much. You obviously work too much. You need to relax."

Sighing, she tucked herself against him again. "Are you going to help me?"

"Me. The music. The margarita." He paused while their server brought another round of drinks, and she picked hers up and sipped. "Just close your eyes."

She did, her lashes fluttering, and he held her there. The alcohol and the music loosened her inhibitions, and he kept her close and warm until she felt as malleable as liquid melting into his bones.

He waited another minute, then slipped his hand beneath her skirt and settled his palm on her thigh. She gasped softly, but he squeezed her shoulder and murmured a calming, "Shh."

Her skin was hot, and he slid his hand higher, urging her with his fingers to part her legs. She did, adjusting her skirt and the tablecloth, and shifting in her seat with a tiny little moan.

The sound she made nearly undid him, but he held on, finding the elastic band of her panties where they sat low on her belly, and easing his fingers beneath. Her sex was swollen and wet, her folds plump, her clit hard.

He toyed with her until her breathing grew ragged, her skin clammy, her pussy wetter than before. And then he reached lower, dipped in and out in a short teasing stroke before he pushed two fingers inside.

Her hand shook, her drink sloshing close to the rim. He watched her bite at her lip, hide her mouth behind the glass. Her eyelids came down, her tongue came out; he wasn't sure if he wasn't feeling her pleasure the more than she was.

His own body tight and aching, he thumbed her clit, rubbing where he knew she wanted the pressure, driving his fingers inside of her while his cock ached at the thought of her heat.

Seconds later she gave a sharp gasp and set her drink on the table, dropping her hand to his thigh. Her muscles contracted and she squeezed him, holding on while she shuddered, and grinding against his hand.

It was all he could do to hold her in her chair. And then she was done, blowing out a long slow breath as he pulled his hand free and sat back.

He was ready to burst. He needed a minute. He'd talk to her then, but Milla had other things on her mind. She turned into his body, crossed one knee over the other and caught his calf with her heel, spreading his legs.

Her hands made quick work of his belt buckle and zipper, and stopping her never crossed his mind. He groaned as she lifted him free from his boxers, and he thanked the club's designer for arranging the tables so that no one could see them when Milla went down.

He sat with one arm draped along the back of her chair. His other hand gripped the edge of his seat. She ran her tongue over and around the head of his cock, sucking him between his lips until he wanted to die.

Her fingers locked around his shaft, and she pressed her thumb to the seam beneath his slit, licking the moisture that oozed there before swallowing him whole.

And that was it. He couldn't hold back. He couldn't wait anymore. He shot everything he had into her throat. He couldn't even give her a warning.

She stayed with him until she'd finished him off, and then she sat up and reached for her drink while he tucked himself back into his pants.

Finally he was able to look over and meet her gaze. She smiled at him from behind her glass, her eyes soft and melting and sexy. "If that's what you meant by relaxing, I could definitely get used to it."

"You're not the only one," he said, and she laughed so hard she and her drink both collapsed in his lap.

15

ON THANKSGIVING MORNING when Hector knocked on the Soons' front door, Angie's mother was the one who answered. It surprised him, seeing her, like he'd forgotten she lived there or something.

He swallowed hard and tried to keep his smile on. "Hello, Mrs. Soon? I'm Hector Prieto. I work at Bergen's with Angie. Your daughter? I'm here to pick her up to go to dinner?"

Angie's mother was even smaller than Angie was. Dainty and fragile-looking, like she'd shatter into a million pieces if the heavy door knocked against her. The fact that it looked as if it was about to do just that, bouncing on its hinges in the wind, made him nervous.

He started to reach out to hold it open. When he did, the older woman returned his smile, and he came to realize that it was only her body and not her spirit that was tiny. She had a whole lot of her daughter in her.

Her eyes flashed brightly, and she spread her arms wide in welcome. "Come in, Hector Prieto. Come in. I am sorry I wasn't here to meet you the night you called for Angela before."

Cripes. He'd almost forgotten about the apple crisp. "Thank you for the dessert. It was great."

She waved off his compliment, wrapping an aqua-colored sweater tightly over her flowery dress. "I'm not much of a cook, but anyone can turn on the oven, slice apples into a dish with brown sugar and cinnamon and crumble butter and oatmeal on top."

The way she described it, he thought even he might be able to make it himself. And then he realized all he smelled were burning candles. He didn't smell any sort of food being cooked, and he was pretty sure Thanksgiving dinner took a long time to put together.

"Mrs. Soon, it's none of my business, but you're not spending today alone, are you? Angie and I don't have to go to the Bergens,'" he added as she closed the door behind him and turned the lock.

"We could stay here with you," he added. "Or we could all three go out to a restaurant. Or you could even come with us. The Bergens, they put on a big feast every year, and they love having a lot of people around."

All Angie's mother did was pat his arm before leading him through the small living room and into the kitchen where she sat at the table with a cup of tea and a *New York Times'* crossword puzzle. He wondered if Angie brought them home when she threw out past issues of the paper at the shop.

"Would you like tea, Hector? I am happy to brew you a cup while you wait for Angela."

He shook his head. Even tea would take up too much of the room he was saving for Mrs. Bergen's cranberry relish. "No, ma'am. I'm fine. But—"

"Well, at least sit then," she said, still not giving him an answer. "Angela shouldn't be long."

He sat, but only on the very edge of the chair. He wasn't comfortable with Angie leaving her mother alone. He wasn't comfortable with himself for not asking before if going to the Bergens was what she really wanted to do.

He hadn't thought about her having other obligations. He was too used to being on his own. "Mrs. Soon—"

"I want to tell you something about Angela," she said, tapping her pencil's eraser on the table. "She is a good daughter. She is the daughter every mother should have. But her father died when she was fourteen, and she has not left my side since. Oh, she goes to work, and she goes to bingo with me and her auntie June, but she does nothing for herself, Hector. Do you understand what I mean?"

He thought he might. He was pretty sure that he did. He nodded. "She told me it's important to her to take care of you. I know she loves you a lot."

"I know that she does. Just as I love her." Mrs. Soon looked down at the folded newspaper, scratched several lines in the corner. "But I don't need her to take care of me. I have this house. I have my sister nearby. I have my husband's death benefit."

Hector heard one door open in the back of the house, listened while another door closed. "From what Angie has said to me, I don't think she knows that."

The older woman bobbed her head. "She knows. I tell her all the time. But she won't let herself believe it."

"I don't know her all that well—"

"She told me she has worked with you for three years," she said, and sat back, pulling her sweater tighter, as if she didn't believe he would be here for her daughter if he didn't know her well.

Hector shrugged. "I'm mostly in the garage and she's in the showroom. When we went to dinner the other night, it was the first time we'd talked away from work."

Two dark brows went up. "Has she told you about her father?"

He shook his head. He wasn't sure he wanted to know that much just yet.

"Angela adored her father. He was her very best friend. His approval meant everything to her. And she nurtured him. She brewed his tea every morning before he went to work. She made sure his magazines were on his reading table every night when he came home."

Mrs. Soon paused to smile. "That man spent more money on subscriptions than he did on gasoline for his car. He never watched television, but he and Angela read his magazines together every night."

"She must miss him a lot." It seemed like such a stupid thing to say, but it was all Hector could think of. He knew about missing family.

Angie's mother nodded. Her expression grew soft and a little bit sad. "He was a wonderful father, but he let Angela do too much. It made her feel needed, he said."

Hector thought back to Angie perched on the edge of his couch, thought back to her saying something about wondering if she could live on her own.

"It's time someone took care of her, Hector," Mrs. Soon said. "It's time someone needed her."

He was saved from having to respond to her mother by Angie walking into the kitchen. She was so pretty, she stole every bit of his breath. He pushed to his feet, taking in the way her dark pink skirt hugged her hips and her legs, the way the neckline of her soft white sweater dipped low enough, but not too low.

Her shoes matched her skirt, the heels as high as always, and for the first time he remembered seeing, she'd pushed her hair from her face with a headband, leaving the length uncoiled.

He couldn't believe it. It fell to her hips, and the strands shone as if they'd been washed and dried in the sun. He grinned, feeling his chest expand, knowing he looked as goofy as hell and not caring at all that he did.

"I wondered once before if your favorite color was pink," he finally said, enjoying the light that flashed in Angie's eyes when he did.

"I don't know why you would think that, Hector. I usually wear blues and greens."

He decided not to tell her about seeing her bra. Instead he told her what was bothering him. "Angie. I was asking your mother if she wanted to come to the Bergens' with us. Rennie's folks won't mind, and I'd hate to leave her here all alone."

"I asked her the same thing last night," Angie said, gesturing with one hand. "But she's going to a turkey buffet with Auntie June later, and then going to the movies, if you can believe it."

Mrs. Soon got to her feet, carried her empty cup and saucer to the sink. "And why wouldn't he believe it, Angela? Tell me what woman in her right mind wouldn't love to spend at least one Thanksgiving day in her life doing nothing but things for herself."

Angie shrugged, and Hector smothered a laugh, turning to follow her and her mother through the kitchen and to the front door where the two women shared a kiss and a hug and a long sweet look.

"I want the two of you to have a wonderful day in the company of your friends," Mrs. Soon said. "June and I will be having our own great fun stuffing our faces with turkey and popcorn. Now go. And I don't want to see you before tonight, dear daughter."

The door closed behind them and Hector followed Angie down the stoop to the sidewalk, catching up with her and taking her hand as they walked to his truck. He smiled when Angie laced their fingers together. "I'm glad I got to meet your mother."

"I'm sure she told you all sorts of things about me that I didn't want you to know," Angie said, tucking close to his side, his arm grazing her breast.

He frowned, concentrating on her words instead of on how her body felt. "Why would you not want me to know things about you? I've told you things about me that no one else knows."

"Really?" she asked, her steps slowing. "Those things about your village? And your cousin?"

He nodded, his throat growing thick. "Ren knows about it, but he's the only one. I just haven't felt like sharing that stuff before now."

"Before me, you mean?" And when he nodded again, she asked, "Why would you want to share it with me?" By now, Angie had come to a complete stop.

Hector looked around. The street was fairly empty. He figured most people were busy with the day's cooking and traveling, and there shouldn't be too many around left to snoop.

He took hold of her arm and guided her the rest of the way to where he'd parked his truck. Then he backed her into the passenger door and stared down into her face.

"Why wouldn't I want to share things with you?" he asked, watching her eyes go wide. "Look what you've done for me. In just a few weeks, look at everything you've done."

"I haven't done much at all," she said softly, checking her headband, pushing back her hair.

He lifted several of the long strands, let them fall through his fingers like rain. "You've thought about me. You've brought me food. You made my home more comfortable. You let me talk about things that have bothered me for a very long time, and you didn't tell me I was stupid for giving most of my money away."

"You're not stupid, Hector. Why would I say that?"

She shook her head, and her dark eyes grew worried and damp. "Caring about your family and wanting to do right by them isn't stupid at all."

He waited a minute, thinking about what her mother had told him, figuring the best way to say what he said next. "Then how come we both do a good job of taking care of everyone but our own selves, Angie? Do you have an answer for that?"

She glanced down, but he lifted her chin. He didn't want her looking anywhere but at him when she answered. Her lip trembled slightly when she reached for the courage and did. "Maybe because it seems selfish to do that when other people need us more?"

"But what if they don't need us more?" He hated saying this stuff, but it just wouldn't stop coming. "What if we just think that they do because it's easier?"

"Easier than what?" she asked, tears filling her big dark eyes.

"Easier than facing our own feelings," he said, having ached so long at having failed his family. "No matter how much money I send home, it's not going to find my cousin. And no matter how much you do for your mamma, it won't bring back your dad."

Angie sniffed but didn't break the hold of his gaze. Neither did she shake loose his hand. She held it instead, reaching up and wrapping her fingers around his wrist.

She squeezed him, closed her eyes ever so briefly. "I told you before, Hector. I don't know if I can live on my own. If I can be by myself."

"You don't have to be by yourself, Angie," he said,

surprising himself with what he was feeling, but knowing it felt good and felt right. "You can be with me."

"Live with you?" she asked. "Is that what you're saying?"

He shook his head. It wasn't time for that. "No. Just be with me. Get to know me. Let me get to know you. See if we're good together." He stroked his thumb over her chin, then over her lower lip. "I think we might be."

She nodded, smiled when he moved his hand around to her neck, closed her eyes when he lowered his head.

He kissed her. Pressed his lips to hers gently, not wanting to scare her, or to rush her, or to force her to do anything she didn't want.

She kissed him back, reaching up to wrap her arms around his neck and pull him even closer than he was. When she parted her lips, he did the same. And when he touched his tongue to hers, she sighed.

It was the best kiss he'd ever had in his life. It was sweet and deep. It meant so much and said everything.

Angie angled her head one way, increasing the pressure of her hands and her mouth. He came back just as hard, tasting her, wanting her, finally pulling away and resting his forehead on hers.

"Is that a yes?" he finally asked once his body had calmed. "You think we might fit?"

She nodded. She smiled. She stole his heart. "I think we fit perfectly, Hector. I think we really do."

MILLA ARRIVED at the Bergen residence at twelve-thirty. The holiday meal was scheduled for one. She didn't see Rennie right away, so headed for the kitchen where she knew she'd find his mother. She was right.

Majorie Bergen's brown eyes went wide with pleasure and surprise. "Why, Milla Page. It has been entirely too long. When Ren told me you two had crossed paths again, I insisted he bring you to Thanksgiving. I'm so glad that for once he did what I asked him to do."

Smiling, Milla stepped into the older woman's embrace, remembering so well the warmth of Rennie's mother. Marjorie didn't seem to have aged at all, though she was finally sporting strands of white in her jet-black hair.

Marjorie was a rock, whether running her household, stepping in when the business needed an organizational hand, or keeping her four sons on the straight and narrow during the years before they left home and established themselves and their careers in different parts of the country. Rennie had called her an intimidating marshmallow, a description that had always made Milla laugh.

"I was thrilled that he asked me," she said, realizing her words were true now even if she'd been less certain at the time. She pulled back to meet Marjorie's kind gaze. "Except it wasn't so much an invitation as it was an order, if you know what I mean."

Marjorie picked up a wire whisk, handed it to Milla and instructed her to stir the gravy that had just started to warm. "I've been dealing with Mr. Bossy for thirty years. I can well imagine that he gave you little choice."

"He's not so bad," Milla said, waving hello to a

third woman talking to a fourth as the duo made their way around the kitchen's large island. "Putting up with Rennie's demands is a small price to pay to be here. I don't know anyone who does up the holiday better."

Marjorie spread napkins in two bread baskets. "I just hope we're not taking you away from celebrating with your own family."

In this case and to this woman, admitting the truth didn't hurt at all. "My parents are spending the week in Aspen, and no doubt enjoying a fabulous meal and even more drink at the lodge."

"They left you alone? On Thanksgiving?"

It was the same reaction she'd received from Natalie and Amy when the two women had insisted separately she join them for the day. "Well, we never have been big on doing things as a family."

"But Thanksgiving." Marjorie clucked her tongue. "I understand parents wanting their children to be independent, but Thanksgiving…"

While Rennie's mother welcomed new arrivals and attended to other chores, Milla stirred the gravy and tried to remember the last time she had spent the holiday with her folks.

Even during college she'd chosen to stay home at least twice, preferring the company of her friends to a long weekend dealing with crowded airports, her mother's bottomless wineglass and the never-ending buzz of her father's cell phone. None of that had been her idea of family fun.

Derek's parents had at least had the meal catered at

their home. But Milla had bowed out of those dinners when possible, opting for the boisterous fun she had with her friends—the sort of fun she could hear being had now in the Bergens' huge great room.

When one of Rennie's sisters-in-law offered gravy duty relief, Milla handed off the whisk and left the bustling kitchen that smelled of turkey, sage, pumpkin and cloves, and made her way down the hall.

At least a dozen men and as many children faced a big-screen TV in the room that served as a den and dining room. Some sat in chairs, some sprawled on the floor, and some perched on the backs of the sofas instead of the seats.

There must have been five or six conversations going on; she couldn't follow a one. She looked for Rennie, finding Hector sitting on the hearth, the petite Asian woman named Angie close to his side, but seeing no other familiar faces.

Not at first, anyway. And then when she did, the face she saw wasn't in the room but taking up a good fifty-two inches of television screen. It was Rennie. He was walking through the Bergen garage and obviously talking to the TV audience since there was no one else around.

She stood in the back of the room, her gaze riveted to the screen. Moments later, Hector appeared, and then another five or six men joined them. The camera followed Rennie as he circled the vehicle they appeared to be working on.

She wasn't sure what it was, though it looked like

it had once been a truck. And then the credits began to roll, the final shot that of the grill of an old Chevrolet, and an upward pan to the hood painted with flames and the words "Hell on Wheels."

It was a show. Rennie's show. It had nothing to do with his bedroom skills, and didn't she feel like a fool? He hadn't told her who he was. She could not believe he hadn't told her *who* he was.

All this time they'd spent talking about their past, talking about honesty and truth, and he had never so much hinted that his working with cars was anything at all out of the ordinary.

She stood there, her eyes glued to the television screen, her feet refusing to move, her head swimming. She wanted to scream. She wanted to break glass objects. She wanted to do both in a very big way.

Instead she turned away calmly and headed for the door, plowing smack into Rennie's chest when she did. She brought up her fists to push him away. He grabbed her and held her still when she fought against his hold.

"It's what I do," he said, and nothing more.

What he did. *What he did?* This was *not* about what he did. This was about who he was, and all the things he hadn't told her. How he hadn't thought it important that she know his full story, or that of their reversal of fortunes. How he had kept from her something this vitally important yet shared it with everyone else in his social circle. God, where was a hole in the floor when she needed one?

"Rebuilding engines? Restoring old cars? Doing

bodywork?" She shook her head. She couldn't decide if she was thrilled by his success, or furious at his deception, or too humiliated to live. "You left out the part about being a TV star."

His dark brows came down in a deep slash. "It's not important."

"Not important?" She felt herself going numb, and she jerked her hands free. She didn't want to feel anything right now. She didn't want to hurt. "You didn't have to see the world to make your millions, did you? You made them right here."

He didn't answer. He didn't say anything at all. Fine. Let him be that way. She'd driven herself here. She could drive herself home. Her purse was locked up in her car, and her keys were in her skirt pocket. She had no reason to stick around, and spun away.

Rennie grabbed her upper arm and walked her through the open front door. But instead of letting her leave, he guided her toward the garage—or what had once been a garage. It was now a game room, and it was filled with kids. He ordered them out, playfully swatted a grumbling nephew on the backside before locking the door.

And then he turned to her and said, "We need to talk."

"Are you sure you're not all talked out?" she heard herself asking, throwing the words back at him that he'd tossed her way before. "I mean, we've done nothing but talk for three weeks now. Well, talk and do that other thing that we can't seem to stop doing."

"There's a reason we can't stop it, Milla." He walked toward her. "You know what it is. So do I."

She circled a large billiards table, backed into a sofa that faced a screen flashing images of an abandoned video game. Their sex life wasn't what mattered here. All she cared about right now was Rennie's monstrous lie.

"You promised. I promised. That we would be honest with each other." She curled her hands into the plush navy fabric on either side of her hips. "This is not being honest."

Rennie hung his head, reached back and rubbed a hand over his neck. "I wasn't ready for you to know. Not when I couldn't get a clear picture of why you'd come to see me."

She stiffened. "You think this is why I came to see you? Because you're rich and famous? If money mattered to me, I wouldn't have signed my trust fund over to my parents."

His head came up. His eyes darkened. "You did what?"

She shook her head. She didn't want to get into that now. "Never mind. Nothing. I just can't believe you thought I was after your money."

This time he scrubbed both hands down his face. "I didn't think you were after my money, Milla."

"Then what? What? Why would you keep something like this from me?"

"I had to be sure that you had come for me. The me you knew. The me you had loved. Not the me everyone else knows. The one from the show."

It made sense and yet it hurt. Damn, but it hurt so much. Thinking that he couldn't trust her? That he couldn't be sure? Her knees shook. She felt her legs threaten to give way, felt her traitorous heart switch sides.

And then she wanted to laugh. She'd said he meant nothing to her. In front of all their friends at the party, she'd said he meant nothing at all.

How could he be sure of anything?

She walked around the end of the monstrous sofa, sinking into the cushions that were still warm from the gamers Rennie had run from the room.

She didn't know what to say. Didn't know what to do. He'd told her he'd forgiven her for her betrayal. But he obviously wasn't going to forget.

Moments later he joined her, sitting right beside her, leaving her no air to breathe that didn't smell of him, making it impossible to escape.

"Most families watch football on Thanksgiving," he said, obviously feeling the need to explain. "The Bergen clan watch 'Hell on Wheels.' It's such a tradition, that I didn't think about it when I asked you here. This isn't how I would have wanted you to find out."

"Would you have told me?" she asked, staring at their knees where they touched, feeling so small when she thought about everyone here knowing but her. "Ever?"

He sighed, draped an arm over her shoulders and pulled her into the curve of his chest. "Yes. I just hadn't figured out the best way."

She plucked a string from the knee of his pants. "You had to see what would happen between us first?"

"No. It's like I said. First I had to see that you were here for me. Not for that guy on television."

"I didn't even know about that guy on television."

"I know that now. I didn't know that then." He rubbed his hand up and down her arm. "There's something else I know that I really need to tell you, but my mother is going to ring the dinner bell any minute, and I need more time than that. Let me take you out Saturday."

"On a date?" One where he'd tell her he'd enjoyed seeing her again, but their baggage was to heavy to carry?

"You and me. No business. Can you wait for me until then?" he asked, nuzzling his cheek to her hair.

She nodded. She could wait for him forever. Even after all the lies, she never doubted that truth.

16

AFTER PICKING UP Milla on Saturday night, Rennie drove her across town to the bar he'd chosen for their date. It was a small neighborhood joint near Bergen Motors with an upstairs pool hall. Neon beer signs and framed photos of the locals were the only decoration.

He'd wanted to take her someplace where he was just a regular Joe, not a star. A place she wouldn't feel compelled to review even if she was off the clock.

Dub's seemed to fit the bill, as did Milla's ass in blue jeans. Damn if she didn't look good, walking in front of him as he guided her to the far corner table. She slid into one side of the booth. He took the other.

Sitting across from her was the only way to guarantee he'd keep his hands to himself. He couldn't risk a repeat of what they'd done last Friday night; Dub's wasn't that kind of club.

He watched her as she flipped through the table's stack of beer coasters, then he glanced over her head toward Butch, the bartender, raised two fingers, shook them twice, added a final thumbs-up.

When he looked back it was to find Milla studying

him, her expression curious, her head cocked to one side. "Is that some sort of baseball signal? Like two out and two on or something?"

He laughed and raised his two fingers again. "It's two beers—" shook them "—two burger baskets—" held up his thumb "—all the way. Is that okay?"

"I'm too impressed that you can signal your order to care," she said, her eyes as wide as her smile.

"C'mon, now." He wiggled both brows. "The magic in these hands can't come as a surprise."

She fought a grin, tried to glare, failed on both accounts and dropped her head back against the top of the booth. "I can't remember the last time I sat and had a beer just for fun."

"That's why I dragged you out of your comfort zone and into mine," he said, realizing his mistake when her head jerked up.

The dark green Naugahyde squeaked beneath her jeans as she scooted forward on the seat, leaning toward him. "My comfort zone? What, is that some sort of reverse social snobbery?"

"I was talking about your work, Milla," he said, though he did file away her accusation to examine later. He might be guilty. He didn't know. "I wanted you to enjoy yourself without having to be on."

She frowned. "Be on?"

How deep was he going to have to dig to get himself out? "You know. On. Thinking like a reviewer."

"MatchMeUpOnline caters to singles from all walks of life." She gave him the company spiel as the waitress brought over their two mugs of draft beer and winked at him before heading back to the bar. "Not all of our clients are looking for the sort of atmosphere you saw in the places we went. And what was that wink all about?"

"That was Jeanie. Dub's daughter. I knew her in high school. And I thought your advertisers wanted edgy," he said, wrapping his hand around his mug.

"They do. But giving them edgy doesn't mean we don't offer more." She ran a finger around the rim of her mug before lifting it to her mouth. "Besides, I always think like a reviewer. Just as I'm sure you always think like someone who's…hell on wheels."

He watched her drink, wondered how he should respond, realized he was impatient to get things between them settled. "Are you okay with the show thing? Or am I still in the doghouse for not being up front?"

She threaded her fingers through the handle of the mug, seeming to pick up on his mood. "I understand why you didn't tell me right away. I don't have to like it, but I do understand."

Somehow, that didn't make him feel any better. "It just seemed like one more thing we'd have to deal with when we already had so many."

"Except that it's who you are," she said, reaching across the table to quickly squeeze his hand. "It's out there. It's you. It's not a hobby or a job tiding you over until you decide what you want to do with your life."

He'd been toying with the edge of his coaster, but glanced up at that. "Is that what you think about your job? That it's just something keeping you busy until you figure things out?"

She grumbled beneath her breath. "Am I that transparent?"

Yes. "No. It just doesn't seem like you love this dating service thing."

She blinked, the light from the lamp hanging low over their table turning her lashes into spiky shadows on her cheeks. "I'm twenty-eight years old. You'd think I'd have figured it out by now."

"Not if you never had the chance."

She lifted her gaze. "I've had six years."

"Yeah, but how long did you spend thinking that you'd graduate, get married and join your parents' country club?" he asked, sitting back as Jeanie returned carrying two burgers in baskets piled high with fries.

Instead of answering, Milla stared down and groaned. Then she reached for the ketchup bottle. "I'll never eat all of this, but I'm damn sure going to try."

He loved how she made him laugh, and got a huge kick watching as she dug in. The look on her face was priceless, and he felt his heart swell. "Good stuff, huh?"

"Oh, my God, you have no idea. I can't remember the last time I ate real French fries." She shivered, moaned, wiggled a little in her seat. "It's like I get to eat the most amazingly delicious food when I'm working, but I'm a burger-and-fries girl at heart. It drove my parents crazy when I'd beg for fast food."

He tried to remember what he'd seen her eat in college. "Did you do it a lot?"

She nodded fiercely. "Oh, all the time. This was when I was pretty little. Before my girlfriends started hating me for eating anything I wanted and never gaining a pound. Of course, I hated them for their boobs."

When he cringed, she laughed. "Hey, you may like them, but even so. They're terribly unfashionable. Just ask Natalie."

"I do like them." He set down his burger after taking a bite. "Natalie. You work with her, right?"

Milla took a swallow of beer and nodded. "Also one of my best friends. She's in charge of the Web site's fashion pages. And a lot of my dates."

He remembered now. Natalie had a fiancé with friends. "Have you ever gone out with someone you've met through the site?"

"A client? No." She glanced back at her food, toyed with a fry. "I actually haven't dated romantically for quite a while."

A buzz settled in to stir at the base of his spine. "How long?"

"Since college," she said without hesitation.

The buzz turned into a stabbing burn. "You haven't dated since then? At all?"

"I've dated, casually, but I haven't been in a relationship," she admitted, picking up her burger and taking a bite.

She was so gorgeous. So animated. "It's hard to believe you haven't found anyone."

"I haven't been looking," she said around a mouthful of food, reaching for her napkin. "And if you have any kind of smarts, these last few weeks should tell you why."

"I haven't been looking, either," he heard himself admit, knowing exactly what she was talking about. "I thought it was because I was busy with the show—"

"Or busy balancing the groupies?"

He shook his head, reached for his beer. "Trust me. I don't do the groupies. None of us do. Jin's married, and Hector's always working. Even if he wanted to, he doesn't have time."

"I saw him on Thanksgiving," Milla said. "With a really cute girl."

Rennie didn't want to talk about his employees. He leaned toward the table, reached across and took hold of her wrist.

This was it. It was time. He was done waiting. "It's all on the table, Milla. Our past. Our present. The fact that neither one of us has even looked to someone else for a relationship."

She pulled free from his hold, then turned her hand over and laced their fingers together. Her eyes were a brighter green than he'd ever seen, the color clear even through her tears. "I'm scared to death, Rennie. We share so much passion, but then we turn around and argue—"

"That's passion, too, Milla," he said, the blade in his back driving deep enough to tear him apart. "It's not like we can turn it off."

"But what if that's all there is?" she asked softly. "What if all we have is—"

"Sex?" When she nodded, he shook his head, fighting frustration and sorrow. "Do you really believe we would have waited for each other if there was nothing between us but sex?"

"Waited?" she asked, toying with the tips of his fingers that had gone cold as if she feared meeting his gaze. "Is that what we've done?"

He didn't answer her. Not then. Not until she couldn't stand the wait and finally had to look up.

"It's what I've done," he said. "It's what I've done."

She choked on a desperate sob, brought his hand to her mouth and kissed his fingers.

He ached with how much he loved her, how much he wanted to make her his wife. How much he wanted to spend his life proving to her that the wait had been worth it.

But he couldn't find enough of his voice to say anything but, "C'mon."

He slid from the booth still holding her hand, and led her to the tiny dance floor in the corner of the bar, while the jukebox played a song about lost loves found.

He wrapped her arms around his neck, wrapped his around her waist and began to move, swaying slowly side to side. When she pressed her face to his chest, he moved one hand to her head to hold her there.

He wanted her as close as he could get her. He didn't even mind when her tears wet his shirt. In fact, he blinked back a few of his own. The emotion between them made talking impossible, made it even harder to breathe.

A month ago he'd thought his life was perfect, thought he had everything he needed, thought that one day a comfortable relationship might be nice but he wouldn't lose any sleep over it happening.

He'd forgotten about Milla's spark. How she didn't let him get away with anything. How she made him a better man. How she brought him to life and made him think. Made him feel.

What he'd felt a month ago was nothing compared to what he felt now. The music stopped, but he didn't let her go. Instead he threaded his fingers into her hair and looked down into her eyes.

"I love you, Milla," he said, his heart lodged in his throat.

She smiled up at him, stealing away the rest of his breath. "I love you, too."

There was only one thing left to settle. "So where do we go from here?"

"WHOEVER DROPPED Michael Foreman's card into the boot? I owe you my undying gratitude." Marian White, the booty call sister who had the floor held up an index finger. "And, I might even be willing to negotiate visitation with our firstborn child."

The small group of women who had gathered in the Wentworth-Holt building's second-floor ladies' room lounge following the Thanksgiving holiday, whooped it up at Marian's announcement.

Milla realized that it had been a while since she'd

seen the zaftig brunette who'd temped at the front desk of the day spa, Indulgence, before moving to the travel agency to work with Jo Ann Green. This romantic development was obviously why Marian had been missing.

"That's so fabulous." Milla's relationship with Rennie was going so well that she wanted everyone to be as happy as she was. "Though I'll opt out of visitation rights, if you don't mind. I didn't drop the card, but neither am I quite ready for kids."

"That's right," said Mercedes Estevez, the exotically sultry owner of Indulgence who'd recently made her own love match. "I heard that things were going well for you, too."

"If they were going any better, you probably wouldn't be able to stand me," Milla admitted with a laugh.

Wearing another pair of animal-skin pumps, Teena growled from the corner of the sofa. "Honey, some of us can't stand you now with that skinny ass and that icy-blond hair."

"Ah, Teena," her coworker Pamela put in, pushing away from the wall to sit on the sofa's arm. "It's not kind to hate those who are less fortunate. Especially when she has the balls to keep it real, and some of us do not."

Milla laughed along with rest of the women, wondering for not the first time how much of their collective obsession with their looks had nothing to do with men. Women were too often their own worst enemies.

She loved that Rennie didn't want her to change a

thing. When he'd driven her home on Saturday night, he'd turned down her invitation to stay over. He hadn't even come inside. He'd walked her to the top of the stairs and that had been as far as he'd gone.

Well, he had kissed her. And she'd spent the rest of the weekend reliving everything about the way that he had. She didn't think a kiss had ever told her so much.

This one let her know how much he'd missed her, how much she meant to him, how long he'd waited, how he would never hurt her again or let her get away.

She'd told him the same things, pressing her lips to his softly, curling her fingers into his T-shirt while he'd cupped her face in his hands.

And God, but seeing him again in a T-shirt and jeans had nearly killed her. Sitting across from him in the booth at Dub's and then dancing with him all snuggled up...

She still couldn't believe she'd managed to keep her hands to herself there on her landing, or that she'd ended up in bed alone. At least she'd had that dance. She sighed. He loved her. God, he loved her.

Could life be any more sweet?

"Milla? Yo, Milla, sweetie?"

The tone of Natalie's voice made it clear that this wasn't her first attempt to get Milla's attention. "Sorry. I was thinking."

"Daydreaming's more like it," Marian teased.

"Looked to me like she was floating," Teena put in before Pamela added, "That's the face of a girl fantasizing about a very special man."

"Guilty, guilty, guilty," Milla said with a laugh, turning back to Natalie. "What's up?"

"Your butt better be in about two shakes." Natalie bumped a hip against the back of Milla's chair. "There's a man here to see you."

Milla frowned. She didn't have any appointments. "In the office?"

"Nope. Downstairs. Outside."

"What—" was all Milla got out before Natalie smacked her in the midsection with her purse.

"You might need that," she said, her brow arched as she fought to keep a straight face.

Just then, the door to the lounge slammed open and Cherie, the Dillard intern, burst in. "You are not going to believe it. That guy from that show 'Hell on Wheels'? He's downstairs. Right now."

Milla's gaze shot from Cherie back to Natalie, and at her girlfriend's knowing nod, she squeaked. "He's here?"

Gesturing wildly and nearly breathless, Cherie hurried on. "He's got this massive RV parked right in front of the building. He's blocking traffic and everything. People are waving and honking. It's insane!"

Milla was out the door and down the hallway before anyone could say another word. When the elevator wasn't fast enough, she turned to head for the stairs, stopping when Natalie called, "Milla, wait."

Rennie was here. With an RV. She couldn't wait. "I've got to go, Nat. I've got to go."

"I know you do, girlfriend. I want you to go. And I

don't want you to look back." When Milla frowned, Natalie went on, her eyes misting. "Don't worry about a thing. I'll handle it all with Joan. Your man is the only thing that matters."

What was she talking about? "Natalie? What? I don't understand."

"You will. In about two minutes." The elevator doors opened then, and Natalie practically pushed Milla inside. "Go. Go. And love him."

The doors shut then, opening thirty seconds later. It wasn't even enough time for Milla to digest what her girlfriend had said.

She scurried through the lobby toward the front of the building, seeing the huge RV before she even made it all the way outside. Once she had, she careened to a stop.

The thing must have been half a block long. And there, standing on the steps in the open door was Rennie Bergen, the love of her life.

She had no idea that it could hurt so much to smile. She walked toward him slowly, holding her purse to her chest. "What are you doing here?"

"I came for you," he said, stepping from the vehicle onto the curb, lifting a hand to acknowledge a cluster of screaming fans.

She let his words sink in, glanced down the side of the RV that was painted with the "Hell on Wheels" logo. "You came for me in this? What, for lunch? Did I forget?"

He shook his head. "Not for lunch. For the rest of your life."

She couldn't breathe. She swore she couldn't breathe. She was freezing. Burning up. Her heart was going to burst. "I don't get what you're saying, Rennie. What? Tell me. What?"

He walked up to her, his dark eyes bright, his hair long and curling wildly over the collar of the T-shirt he wore with his jeans and his black biker boots.

Before she could say a word, he took her purse from her hands and tossed it onto the RV's steps. And then he did what she'd never in a million years thought she'd see him do.

In front of all of San Francisco, Rennie Bergen, star of "Hell on Wheels" got down on one knee in front of her.

"I love you, Milla Page," he said, his voice a gruff rasp, his eyes red with emotion. "Will you marry me?"

She cried. It was all she could do. Big, fat, sloppy, sobbing hiccups kept her from saying a word. Tears ran like rain down her cheeks. But she nodded. Oh, God, how she nodded.

She was still sobbing and nodding when he dug into his pocket for the ring. Her hand, when he took it in his, was shaking. But he found the finger he wanted, and he slid on the biggest diamond solitaire she'd ever seen.

Then he got to his feet and grinned, and she threw her arms around his neck, and he picked her up and spun her around. "Oh, Rennie. Oh, Rennie, oh, Rennie, oh, Rennie. I love you. Have I told you that today? I love you so very much."

He laughed. A great big laugh that came up out of his gut. "You love me enough to take the first shift driving once we get out of the city?"

Out of the city? What was he talking about? "Where are we going?"

"Anywhere you want to go," he said, finally setting her down.

"What?"

"We don't start filming the new season for a couple of months. I put Hector in charge until then."

"Are you kidding me?"

"Would I be here blocking traffic if I were?"

"What about my job?"

"Natalie's going to take care of that for you."

Milla turned around to see Natalie standing on the sidewalk, Amy waddling up to her side. Both women blew her kisses and waved.

Behind them, she saw Teena and Pamela. Marian and Mercedes. Danica and Tamara who'd joined them. Cherie and Julia and Jo Ann. The sisters of the booty call had come to send her off into her new life. She waved at them all, then turned back to Rennie.

She was marrying this man, the man who she loved, this man who would love her forever. How had she ever thought she could live without him?

"Are you sure you want me to drive?" she asked, reaching out to tickle him. "I've been told I'm hell on wheels."

He grabbed at her hand. "Just see if you can get us to Vegas in one piece. There's a chapel there with our name on it."

"Vegas?" she asked, giggling. "That's the best you can do?"

"Baby? The best is yet to come."

* * * * *

New York Times *bestselling author Linda Lael Miller is back with a new romance featuring the heartwarming McKettrick family from Silhouette Special Edition.*

SIERRA'S HOMECOMING
by Linda Lael Miller

*On sale December 2006,
wherever books are sold.*

Turn the page for a sneak preview!

Soft, smoky music poured into the room.

The next thing she knew, Sierra was in Travis's arms, close against that chest she'd admired earlier, and they were slow dancing.

Why didn't she pull away?

"Relax," he said. His breath was warm in her hair.

She giggled, more nervous than amused. What was the matter with her? She was attracted to Travis, had been from the first, and he was clearly attracted to her. They were both adults. Why not enjoy a little slow dancing in a ranch-house kitchen?

Because slow dancing led to other things. She took a step back and felt the counter flush against her lower back. Travis naturally came with her, since they were holding hands and he had one arm around her waist.

Simple physics.

Then he kissed her.

Physics again—this time, not so simple.

"Yikes," she said, when their mouths parted.

He grinned. "Nobody's ever said that after I kissed them."

She felt the heat and substance of his body pressed

against hers. "It's going to happen, isn't it?" she heard herself whisper.

"Yep," Travis answered.

"But not tonight," Sierra said on a sigh.

"Probably not," Travis agreed.

"When, then?"

He chuckled, gave her a slow, nibbling kiss. "Tomorrow morning," he said. "After you drop Liam off at school."

"Isn't that…a little…soon?"

"Not soon enough," Travis answered, his voice husky. "Not nearly soon enough."

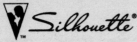

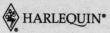

HARLEQUIN®

American ROMANCE®

IS PROUD TO PRESENT

COWBOY VET
by Pamela Britton

Jessie Monroe is the last person on earth
Rand Sheppard wants to rely on, but he needs
a veterinary technician—yesterday—and she's the
only one for hire. It turns out the woman who
destroyed his cousin's life isn't who Rand thought
she was. And now she's all he can think about!

"Pamela Britton writes the kind of
wonderfully romantic, sexy, witty romance
that readers dream of discovering
when they go into a bookstore."

—*New York Times* bestselling author
Jayne Ann Krentz

Cowboy Vet *is available from
Harlequin American Romance in December 2006.*

REQUEST YOUR FREE BOOKS!

2 FREE NOVELS PLUS 2 FREE GIFTS!

HARLEQUIN®

Blaze®

Red-hot reads!

nocturne™

**Explore the dark and sensual
new realm of paranormal romance.**

HAUNTED
BY LISA CHILDS

**The first book in the riveting
new 3-book miniseries, Witch Hunt.**

DEATH CALLS
BY CARIDAD PIÑEIRO

**Darkness calls to humans,
as well as vampires...**

*On sale December 2006,
wherever books are sold.*

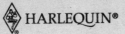

COMING NEXT MONTH

#291 THE MIGHTY QUINNS: DECLAN Kate Hoffmann
The Mighty Quinns, Bk. 3
Security expert Declan Quinn isn't exactly thrilled with his latest job, acting as bodyguard for radio sex-pert Rachel Merrell—until she drags him into her bed and shows him what *other* things he can do to her body while he's guarding it....

#292 SECRET SANTA Janelle Denison, Isabel Sharpe, Jennifer LaBrecque
(A Naughty but Nice Christmas Collection)
Christmas. Whether it's spending sensual nights cuddled up by the fire or experiencing the thrill of being caught under the mistletoe by a secret admirer, *anything* is possible at this time of year. Especially when Santa himself is delivering sexy little secrets....

#293 IT'S A WONDERFULLY SEXY LIFE Hope Tarr
Extreme
Baltimore street cop Mandy Delinski doesn't believe in lust at first sight—at least until she's almost seduced by gorgeous Josh Thornton at a Christmas party. Talk about a holiday miracle! For once it looks as if she's going to get *exactly* what she wants for Christmas—until she finds her "perfect gift" in the morgue the next day....

#294 WITH HIS TOUCH Dawn Atkins
Doing It...Better!
With no notice, Sugar Thompson's business partner Gage Maguire started a seduction campaign...on *her*. That's against all the rules they established years ago. Sure, he's tempting her. Only, it's too bad he seems to want more than the temporary fling she has in mind....

#295 BAD INFLUENCE Kristin Hardy
Sex & the Supper Club II, Bk. 1
Paige Favreau has always taken the safe path. Career, friends, lovers—she's enjoyed them all, but none have rocked her world. Until blues guitarist Zach Reed challenges her to take a walk on the wild side....

#296 A TASTE OF TEMPTATION Carrie Alexander
Lust Potion #9, Bk. 3
After a mysterious lust potion works its sexy magic on her pals, gossip columnist Zoe Aberdeen wants to know the story behind it. When she asks her neighbor—and crime lab scientist—Donovan Shane for help, he's not interested. But thanks to Zoe's "persuasive" personality, he's soon testing the potion and acting out his every fantasy with the sassy redhead....